HARPOON GUNNER

By Bryce Walton

Thomas Y. Crowell Company
New York

By the Author

CAVE OF DANGER
HARPOON GUNNER

To Ruth,
who once dreamed of Zuther Notion

So cheer up, my lads,
Let your hearts never fail
While the bold harpooner
Is striking the whale.

—OLD WHALERS' SONG

ONE

Erik Nordahl walked. He had passed the point of exhaustion long ago, but he stopped only once—to stare into the fog that pressed in around him like wet cotton-wool.

"Go away," he shouted desperately. "Haven't I had enough tough luck already?"

But the fog did not go away. Erik trudged on, fighting a growing sense of panic about his future.

He had run away from forced exile on his Uncle Grimstad's farm, high in the desolate mountains of Telemark. He had not had a krone in his pockets for train or bus fare, and he had hoped to make good time hitchhiking. But autumn rains had flooded roads and washed out bridges, and he had not been able to catch many rides. He'd been forced to walk most of the way to Norway's east coast.

Once he reached the busy coastal road, he'd been

sure he would catch a fast ride to Tönsberg and make up for lost time. Instead his bad luck only got worse. The coastal highway from Oslo to Larvik lay buried in cold autumn fog. It clung to Erik's face, cutting visibility, chilling his bones. Very few motorists dared to drive in such a fog. Those who did passed Erik by, unable to see him a few feet away as he slogged along the shoulder, a thirty-pound pack on his back.

Now he was days behind schedule. He only hoped he wasn't too late. Because this was the year 1967, and he was already sixteen years old, and there was a definite age limit to becoming a whale gunner in *Zuther Notion*.

So he pushed himself harder, his eyes bleary from lack of sleep, his legs aching with tiredness. When he felt as though he might not be able to keep going, he thought of Bornak's letter. It was in his pocket, and he knew the words by heart:

"Dear Erik Nordahl,

"Since I got back from killing whale last June I've been trying to locate you. I asked about you in Oslo and Tönsberg, and I wrote letters to boarding schools and orphanages. Finally I found out what had happened to you—how, after your father was killed, you were shipped from relative to relative like a bale of loose cargo. Now you are a shameful exile on your Uncle Grimstad's farm. That is a very disgraceful place for a prince of gunners to be, lad. No true son of a har-

2

pooner should have to stoop to such humiliating chores.

"When your father was killed by a blue whale last year in *Zuther Notion*, I was with him. Before Egil died, he asked me to help you become a harpooner. 'Give my boy his chance at the whale,' he said to me, and I promised I would. Now I will keep my promise. I will be your patron in *Zuther Notion*. I will take you aboard my catcher, train you, guide you, see that you get your ten required contract shots at whales and gain your gunner's certificate.

"You must, then, leave the farm, and come at once to Tönsberg. Don't worry about your Uncle Grimstad's objections or about the authorities. Trust Bornak of Bygland. But we must be careful. You will be a runaway, a minor, leaving home and going to sea without your guardian's consent. We must take no chances on your getting caught. Be in Tönsberg a week before the *Arcturus* sails, and that will give us time to work out a good safe way to get you aboard.

"Meet me then at the Vestfold Whaling Museum by the skeleton of the big blue whale. Wait there for further word and instructions from me. Until then you must not mention my name or your name or our purpose to anyone.

"I'll have no problem recognizing you, Erik. Your father left me a picture of you. Write back to me at once, care of Seamen's Hall in Tönsberg. Say when you will be at the Whaling Museum ready for the great

3

whale hunt. Until then, *hvalblast!* I remain your father's
and your friend, and your brother harpooner."

"Bornak of Bygland, King of Gunners."

That letter from Norway's most renowned harpooner
had given life again to Erik's great dream of becoming
a harpoon gunner—the dream that had died and been
buried with his father far down in *Zuther Notion.* Erik
had written back at once promising Bornak to be in
Tönsberg a week before the *Arcturus* sailed, and he had
left the farm despite Uncle Grimstad's angry threats. A
promise of help from the most famous of all gunner
heroes, Bornak of Bygland, had made anything seem
possible.

But he was six days late reaching Tönsberg. Worse
yet, upon his arrival there he learned that the factory
ship *Arcturus* was due to sail that very evening, a day
ahead of schedule.

And when he got to the Vestfold Whaling Museum,
carefully avoiding a run-in with the police, he saw no
one who looked at all like the famous Bornak. He knew
he would recognize the great gunner at once if he saw
him, for he had seen Bornak's picture many times.

Erik melted into the crowd of museum visitors and
kept on looking. He stayed in the background and tried
to keep his face hidden from the police who were much
in evidence. He knew there was an alarm out for him

as a runaway. Every policeman would be carrying his description, and would be on the lookout for him.

This day of the whalemen's departure was the most celebrated of the year in the thousand-year-old viking port of Tönsberg. The narrow cobbled streets were crowded with tourists. Many of them visited the Whaling Museum atop Castle Hill, drawn by its main attraction—the skeleton of a giant blue whale.

"A hundred and twenty feet long," explained the guide, "and one hundred and fifty tons! It is the biggest animal the world has ever known, bigger even than the greatest dinosaur that ever thundered over a prehistoric land. This record blue whale, *balaenoptera musculus*, or sulphur-bottom for short, was taken by Norway's champion gunner, Bornak of Bygland."

The awed visitors stared.

Erik wasn't interested. In his patched, mud-spattered clothes he stood at the rear of the crowd. His shaggy hair fell over his face. His rain-sogged rucksack hung from one aching shoulder. He cared only about trying to find Bornak. But, he asked himself, why did he bother? Would the great Bornak wait for him for six days? He probably wouldn't do that even to keep a promise to an old friend.

Still, Erik thought stubbornly, Bornak might have left a message, or he might have sent someone else to look

5

for him. The tour guide might know something. Erik waited for the old man to finish his lecture.

Erik only half listened to the guide's talk. His father had already taught him just about everything there was to learn about whaling. His interest fired up though when the guide pointed at the harpoon gun. Mounted on a black iron base, it was a stubby and vicious-looking Svend Foyn with worn pistol grip and a heavy barbed shaft protruding from the muzzle.

"The gun is fired by powder like a cannon," the guide said. "The harpoon is also loaded with a bomb that explodes inside the whale. This is a far cry from the old days when men hunted whale from small boats using hand-thrown harpoons. Big as it is, I fear the whale has little chance against bomb-throwing artillery like the Svend Foyn."

"He'll have no chance at all," Erik thought, "when I get my sights trained on him." And in his imagination he was already crouched on the bow of a whale catcher behind his Sven Foyn. He was far down in the Antarctic seas taking aim at the back of a giant blue . . . .

The guide's voice brought Erik back to the museum hall. The old man was talking about harpoon gunners now, and he was pointing to the wall where there were bronze plaques, silver award cups, and gold-framed pictures of Norway's gunner heroes.

There was a picture of Erik's father, another of Bornak. His father's picture was small, and compared with

the picture of the great Bornak, it seemed fuzzy and un-
important.

Erik swallowed uneasily. His father's face looking
down at him made him feel an uncomfortable mixture
of sadness and resentment. Why hadn't his father, years
ago, taken him along to *Zuther Notion?* Other gunners
took their sons to the Antarctic when they were no more
than nine or ten years old. At Erik's age they were vet-
eran harpooners, blasting away at big fins and blues.

Erik stared up at his father's silent face. Why didn't
you give me the same break? he thought bitterly. Whatever the reason, Erik knew he was far behind other
gunners his age, and he had to catch up.

The museum guide finally finished his lecture. Erik
asked him if Bornak had left a message, but the old
man answered that as far as he knew, Bornak had not
even been up to the museum this season. "Bornak's
probably aboard the *Arcturus* now," he said. "She's
sailing this evening."

Erik ran out into the hazy afternoon sunlight. He
didn't have much time to find Bornak, but he had to try.
Without Bornak's help he had no chance of shipping
out on the *Arcturus* or any other vessel. He would have
to be very careful, however; he could easily be recognized, picked up by the authorities, and shipped back to
Uncle Grimstad.

Erik knew that his uncle had alerted every port authority, police officer, harbor police, and all the ships' captains in Norwegian ports to be on the lookout for a runaway minor named Erik Nordahl. Erik had no permit to leave home, let alone ship out. If spotted and questioned, he wouldn't have a chance. No one, not even Bornak, could help him if he were picked up by the police.

Still he had to try to find Bornak. If he couldn't sail aboard the *Arcturus,* he cared very little about what happened to him.

Erik hesitated a moment, then started down Castle Hill. To save time, he avoided the congested roadway and took the long flight of wooden steps. Cracked and bleached by the sun and wind, they angled back and forth through a thick growth of trees and bushes interspersed with white wooden houses.

Far below him, down the terraced hills, the usually quiet old whaling port was filled with excitement. Thousands of men were going to the dangerous Antarctic to hunt the whale. Friends and relatives crowded the waterfront. A brass band played at the end of a pier. Motorboats were roaring out from and back to the quay. Colored pennants and the flag of Norway fluttered from every window and masthead.

Part way down the steps, Erik shaded his eyes and tried to find the *Arcturus.* But she was anchored a quarter of a mile out in the Oslo Fjord, hidden by a stubborn fogbank. Thirty-thousand tons, bigger than most ocean liners, she was far too heavy to put in alongside a Tönsberg pier.

Erik started down the steps again, but a sound behind him made him suddenly stop and turn. He looked up. He saw nothing at first as he listened and heard only the wind.

"Erik Nordahl?" A man appeared suddenly at the top of the steps. "Erik Nordahl?" he repeated.

Quickly the man started down after Erik, his boots padding silently on the planks like a cat's.

Erik's stomach went cold. He knew the man coming at him was a cop. He had been recognized up at the museum, he thought, and prepared to vault the rail and run into the concealment of brush and trees.

TWO

"Hold up if you're Erik Nordahl. Bornak sent me."

Erik sagged against the rail with relief. He eased the rucksack from his aching shoulders.

The stranger wore soft-soled boots of hand-sewn sea-elephant hide. He also wore a carefully tailored duffel coat with a sealskin collar, a beret with a red pompon, and a patch over his left eye. His face had been hardened and pitted and burned by sun and seawind until it looked like a chunk of eroded iron.

"Erik Nordahl?" His voice was quick, sharp, impatient. Erik nodded. The single eye fixed him with a steady, mocking curiosity. "Bornak gave me your picture so I would recognize you. Just the same, I almost didn't. Who'd ever guess a prince of gunners would wear that hayseed rig? You're a prince in disguise all right."

Erik quietly returned the man's stare. He knew he was a bit tall and gawky for his age. On top of that, he must really look ridiculous with his corn-shuck hair and clodhopper clothes. He also knew that sailors generally held farmers in contempt, calling them land crabs. But still, Erik reminded himself, Bornak has surely told this fellow that I'm a prince of gunners. He must know that Bornak, a king of harpooners, is my patron. Why the sarcastic tone and mocking grin? This man isn't even a gunner, Erik thought. His hands show no callouses or gunner's scars.

"I'm Tiburon," the one-eyed man said. "Bornak's chief bosun."

"Pleased to meet you," Erik said, as a mere formality. He held out his hand. Tiburon gave it a quick grip, but he was frowning.

"I'd be a lot more pleased to see you if you hadn't shown up a week late. What the devil held you up?"

"Rain, flooded roads, fog," Erik flared angrily. "I had to hitchhike, and I had to stay clear of the police all the way. You think I didn't get here as soon as I could?"

"Police is right," Tiburon said unhappily. "Bornak said you'd be a runaway minor. Now your picture's posted, and it seems as if every officer and his brother are on the lookout for you. That's bad."

"How bad?"

"If you're picked up there's nothing anyone can do to help you—that's how bad. It means you're going to have to be mighty careful getting to the docks and across to the *Arcturus*. It means you're risking a very close haul getting aboard the *Arcturus* and that if you manage to stay aboard her, it'll be a miracle."

"Can Bornak still get me aboard?" Erik asked anxiously.

"Bornak can't do anything to help a runaway minor," Tiburon growled. "He can't help you get aboard or help you stay aboard, if you ever reach the ship. That's strictly up to you, kid."

"But Bornak said he'd help—"

"Sure," Tiburon cut in impatiently. "If you'd gotten here a week ago when you were supposed to, Bornak was going to try to work out some way for you to go aboard in disguise, maybe as a sailor. He might have been able to get you a deck job or something. But it's too late for that now."

"Can't he do anything?" Erik asked.

"What can Bornak do now?" Tiburon raised his hands in mock despair. "Way down in the Antarctic whaling ground, Bornak's a big wheel, the king of gunners. But here among the landlubbers he's just another whaleman. Do you think he can stand up to the port authorities, the local and state police? Don't you know how strict they've gotten about minors shipping out to sea? Why if they caught Bornak or me or any other whaleman helping some underage kid running away to sea, they'd put us away in the lockup for ten years!"

Erik swallowed thickly and struggled to control his feelings. "So wha—what am I supposed to do now?"

12

"Come along with me to the docks," Tiburon said. "There's a way you can get out to the *Arcturus* if we hurry—and if you don't get nabbed by the cops. So stay low and keep your eyes peeled. And get this, kid. If the police spot you and go after you, I'm taking off in the opposite direction so fast you won't even see me. I don't want to be locked up for aiding and abetting a runaway minor. Is that clear?"

"Clear enough," Erik said, and he followed Tiburon down the steps. At the bottom, Tiburon led the way along a narrow road, then through an alley toward the docks.

"How am I to get out to the *Arcturus*?"

"Right now worry about the cops," Tiburon warned, "and about making time." He checked his wristwatch and walked faster. "Your being late has also fouled us up here. Your one last chance to get out to the *Arcturus* will be gone in about twenty more minutes."

Soon Erik was being led down an alley toward the waterfront. The sea winds carried the exciting odors of wet hemp, spices, old pilings, tar, fish, salt, and seaweed. Erik ducked after Tiburon out of the alley and behind a pile of cargo bales.

Tiburon gripped his arm tensely. "There at the end of the pier is a launch that's taking a last load of passengers for a guided tour of the *Arcturus*. That's a sure way for you to get aboard without attracting attention or arousing suspicion. You'll just be another tourist, unless some cop recognizes you. In that case, forget it."

"And when I'm aboard with the touring party, what then?"

"You wait for your chance to sneak away from them without being seen. If you're caught wandering that cargo deck alone and you're picked up and questioned, then you're *kaput*. Remember, Bornak can't help you here, not even aboard ship. He can't help you until we're far down in *Zuther Notion*, in the whaling grounds. There, Bornak has plenty of authority. If you make it that far, Bornak will take care of the rest. But the first step is to get aboard the *Arcturus* and hole up."

Erik's heart beat very fast and he felt his stomach tighten. His voice choked up in his throat. "You mean I—I've got to be a stowaway."

"That's right, kid. Until you get far down into the South Atlantic. Until then you're a stowaway."

"But—a stowaway's the worst thing you can be," Erik whispered. "A whaling captain looks on a stowaway as being lower than a rat or cockroach."

"All the same, that's the way it has to be," said Tiburon, "if you want to get to *Zuther Notion* and become a harpoon gunner."

Erik nodded stiffly. "I—I don't know much about how to be a stowaway."

"You can get some help," Tiburon said, and gave a

14

thin grin. "As soon as you can break away from the
tour party, go to the foredeck, the starboard foredeck.
Door number three in the forward superstructure. Got
that?"

Erik repeated it. Tiburon said, "Bornak or I will meet
you there, and show you where you can hole up until
we get down to the whaling grounds. We'll see that
you get food and water. That's all we can do."

Erik breathed easier. That was better than no help at
all. He peered out between the cargo bales across the
quay and the water of the fjord. Gulls swooped and
cried. Motorboats, sailboats, and launches were heading out into the fogbank. On the docks motor lorries
were crawling out of warehouses, hauling trains of cargo.
Friends and relatives waved good-bye. Women were
tossing wreaths of fresh flowers into the waters of the
fjord. The brass band, the milling crowd, the screaming
of gulls and stormy petrels circling overhead, sharpened
Erik's sense of urgency.

"Get ready now," Tiburon said tightly. "And whatever happens, you'd better not be Erik Nordahl—at
least not until you get far enough south so that Captain Haakonsson can't send you back."

Erik gulped. "I—I can't be myself?"

Tiburon threw up his hands again impatiently. "Look,
kid. Let's say you are caught stowing away, what then?
If they know you're Erik Nordahl, the runaway minor,
you're sure to be shipped home at once and sent away to

15

a work farm as a juvenile delinquent. But if you're someone else, some nobody or other, you have a slim chance of staying aboard even if you are a stowaway. If you're caught, let's say you tell them you're some ignorant nobody of a land crab named Orm Gudmundsen."

Erik grimaced. "Orm Gudmundsen?"

"Right. And let's say you have no identification papers. You tell them you're of legal age, eighteen. They'll have no way of checking. Sometimes they're lenient with stowaways—although they put them through some mighty punishing work. Well, that's settled. From now on until you get to *Zuther Notion*, you're not, nor have you ever been, Erik Nordahl. You're Orm Gudmundsen, dumb country oaf."

Erik nodded heavily. "Orm Gudmundsen, dumb oaf."

"And of course you'll never mention knowing Bornak, or the fact that Bornak has had anything to do with your stowing away," Tiburon warned. "What's in the rucksack, kid?"

"Rations, blanket, some clothes," Erik answered.

"Anything there to identify you as Erik Nordahl?"

"No."

"Name?" Tiburon snapped.

"Ord—er—Orm Nordgood—Gudmundsen—"

"Where do your parents live?"

"I don't have any parents. My mother died when I was born. Father was killed last year."

"Where you from, orphan boy?"

"From up around Lopphavet."

"How old are you?"

"Don't know for sure, sir. Going on eighteen, maybe."

"Ever seen a schoolhouse?"

"Not from inside. I've always had to work. No time for schooling."

"Identification?"

"What?"

"Forget it, orphan boy. You're a farmer with no schooling. Just what good use do you think you could be put to on a whaling ship?"

"Well, I only know that all my life I've dreamed of going whaling. I don't care what work I do or how much, sir. I'll be a bilge swab, pot walloper, blubber-boy, anything. Just as long as I can go whaling, sir."

Tiburon grinned a little. "And you never heard of a prince of gunners named Erik Nordahl?"

"Never, sir."

"You'll do. Are you carrying anything in your pockets that might identify you?"

Erik started to take his school card and some letters, including the one from Bornak, from his wallet. Then he remembered that his initials were on the wallet, and he handed everything over to Tiburon.

"Anything else?"

Erik hesitated, then took off the ring from his left hand, and handed it to Tiburon.

Tiburon whistled as he held it up to the fading light. The ring was set with a ruby stone shaped like a finwhale. "This is quite a prize."

"It was my father's. The people of Tönsberg awarded it to him the year he won his king of gunner's crown. He gave it to me before his last voyage."

Erik thought of the inscription on the outside of the wide gold band: "*To Egil Nordahl, King of Gunners, Tönsberg, 1954.*" And Erik also thought of the other inscription that his father had had cut inside the ring: *To my son, Erik, Prince of Gunners—and one day a king.*

Erik's throat felt a little tight, and he looked away from Tiburon. He heard the bosun's voice say in a softer tone, "Maybe you should hang onto this, kid. Just keep it out of sight somewhere. There's a good chance you'll never make it out on the *Arcturus*—and I guess you'd want to hang on to this ring."

"No," Erik said quickly. "If I can't get aboard the *Arcturus* and stay, the ring won't mean anything."

"You're dead set on being a gunner, aren't you?"

"I'm a Nordahl. And the Nordahls have been gunners for generations."

"I know," Tiburon said, staring out across the fjord.

"All my life I've planned to be a gunner, to hunt and shoot whale. When I was thirteen, my father, Egil Nordahl, took me out on a whale catcher boat, out of Bovaagen Hval, an old shore whaling station on the

Norwegian Sea. He threw inflated rubber rafts into the sea, and I fired at them until I could shoot a harpoon into one almost every time."

Tiburon nodded, but his jaw set in a hard line and his eye darkened and narrowed. "Sure, but you've never seen a hundred tons of whale blowing blood. You've never seen a big part of God's sea turned red as sin. Until you see a bomb shot into a heart weighing half a ton, you don't know anything about whaling."

Erik swallowed slowly. He said nothing.

Tiburon said, "All right, move out now. Try to get to Bornak as soon as you're aboard. Remember starboard foredeck. Door number three in the forward superstructure. Got that?"

Erik repeated it again, and Tiburon told him to go straight out to the end of pier five and to hurry because it was his last chance.

Then Erik was nodding and moving out into the crowd. He thought he heard Tiburon wish him good luck, but he didn't look back as he headed as fast as he could down the wharfside toward pier five.

A voice was blasting through a megaphone at the end of the pier: "Last chance for tour of famous factory ship *Arcturus*. One more free tour before she sails for *Zuther Notion*."

Erik hurried through the crowd. The big passenger launch was tied up at the end of the pier. As one of those visiting tourists, Erik knew that he could walk

launch, the passengers, and everything else but the promise of the *Arcturus* waiting just ahead. He leaned into the spray, squinting and straining his eyes. Gulls wheeled above the flat swells, and scurries of petrels stormed through the clouding sky. Erik gripped the railing hard with both hands and held his breath as he waited. When the giant factory ship at last began to appear, breaking through the mist like gray-blue mountain crags from the clouds, Erik's breath went out in a long sigh. He got an all-round view of the floating factory then as the launch keeled hard right and circled about to come in on the *Arcturus'* lee, free of the wind.

It was a giant ship all right, he thought, designed for many things. It was the mother ship for a great fleet of fourteen vessels and seven hundred men, whom it would have to supply and support for six months in the wastes of the freezing south. It would also take aboard whale carcasses, cut them up, process them, reduce them to oil and bonemeal and a hundred or so other products which it would store in its hold and bring back to Norway at season's end.

It seemed to Erik a freakish hulk, grilled, pocked, humped, with a mad assortment of outsized gadgets, chimneys, ventilation shafts, pipes, beams, winches, hoists, and smokestacks. It had a long, low, open center deck that extended between high fore-and-aft superstructures resembling six-story apartment buildings. This open deck space was piled with mountains of cargo, and

22

it made Erik think more of the cluttered yard of a big manufacturing firm than of a ship.

Maybe the *Arcturus* wasn't a ship, he thought. It had none of a real ship's beauty and grace. It was blunt, blackened, and scarred like some sooty factory that had broken loose from land and was about to drift away to sea.

Ugly, but magnificently ugly all the same; it was the famous old *Arcturus* waiting to take him to high adventure in *Zuther Notion*. He would only be aboard the factory ship a short time in any case. Before long he'd be standing with Bornak on the gunner's deck of a fast whale catcher, cruising the pack ice and shooting away at big finners and blues.

The launch tied up at the floating platform below the gangplank. Whalemen crowded the railing and the cargo deck and waved at the boatloads of women who were circling the ship, still throwing flowers into the water.

A Norski guide led the visitors along the scupperway and shouted at them through a megaphone. Erik soon realized that the guide was leading them in the wrong direction—at least, for Erik's purposes. The guide was walking aft, and Erik had to go forward where he would find Bornak in the forward superstructure. He hung back until he was in the rear of the group, then dropped a few feet behind it. He kept waiting and watching for a chance to slip away unnoticed. He was running out of time.

Acres of open deck were stacked with cargo, some of it in piles twenty-five feet high. Narrow alleyways ran through the cargo, cobwebbed with battening lines of rope, chain, and cable. Bales, crates, barrels, machinery, and great square piles of lumber formed more high walls and alleyways. Once Erik got away into that maze he could escape detection easily enough, but getting away unseen was another matter. He felt that he was being watched. One of the visitors was always glancing his way, or the guide, or some of the deckmen who were moving about checking lines and hatches and handling cargo.

"This fleet," the guide bawled through his megaphone, "is known as Pelagic Whaling Expedition, Number One. Pelagic means seagoing. The entire fleet must be self-sufficient for six months in one of the most uninhabitable regions left in the world. . . ."

"The *Arcturus'* great engines will turn steadily, never stopping, for fifty thousand miles. . . ."

A wind blew up suddenly and whined through the upper rigging. Erik heard it and looked uneasily at the sky turning darker to the northeast. At that moment the guide pointed to port, and every gaze seemed to follow his gesture. Erik took the chance and jumped to the side, into a narrow aisle between ten-foot high walls of wooden crates. He crouched down, holding his breath, and listened for any shout or indication that he'd been seen. Hearing nothing, he hurried to an intersection and darted down a wider aisle.

He forced himself to move slowly to avoid attention. He was running out of time rapidly, and he had to get back along the entire length of the cargo deck to find Bornak. He hurried as fast as he could, but it was difficult enough just to keep angling forward through that unfamiliar maze of cargo. He lost himself, first in a pile of oil drums, then in a confusion of piping. He had to stop often to listen and look ahead and make sure the way was clear. Sometimes he had to jump and crawl into hiding while deckies moved about tightening cables and securing hatches against the rising wind.

Erik had to angle to port, then starboard, waiting, listening, taking circuitous bypaths to avoid being spotted. Finally he backed up hard against a wall of oiled canvas that covered a high pile of crates. Breathing hard and fighting panic, he listened to the rising gale. I should have reached the forward superstructure by this time, he thought. I should have, but I haven't. And where am I now?

A general answer was easy. He was still on the cargo deck. But where? Where on the cargo deck? Surrounded by the walls of supplies rising above his head, he had no idea which way to go to get either forward or aft or to port or starboard. The dark sky overhead told him nothing. The wind, northeasterly when he'd come aboard, had changed direction.

He would have to crawl up on top of the cargo to get his bearings. Risky, he thought, but it was the only way. He started to climb, but a roar from the ship's main deck loudspeaker brought him down again to the deck: "Attention, all ship's hands and visitors. Bad weather is expected soon. We're preparing to get under way to clear the fjord. Will all who are going ashore please report at once to the port gangway immediately. I repeat, attention all ship's hands and visitors. Bad weather is expected soon—"

Erik ran to the side, then angled left. Now he knew what direction was forward. There was no doubt about where that thundering loudspeaker voice had come from. The main speaker was always fixed to the flying bridge of the forward superstructure, above the officers' quarters.

He twisted, backtracked, and cut down another aisle; but this only led him into a tangle of valves, bollards, and thick pipes. Instead of wasting time turning back, he squirmed through twenty feet of this strange jungle gym until he stumbled free. Breathing hard, he forced himself ahead. A few minutes later he was caught in another web of oil drums and machinery. He ran for a moment in a wild, unreasoning circle, then pounded down an aisle that seemed to lead straight into the steel wall of the forward superstructure.

It did, but there was no door number three. There was no door there at all, just riveted plates with chipped paint and rust pits showing an inner erosion. The walls of cargo forming the aisle in which Erik stood were flush with the superstructure wall. The next aisle to the right or left might end in a doorway, and that door might be number three where Bornak waited. He would have to crawl up over the cargo to find out.

He started to move, but the deck seemed to come and go at him in a dizzy way. He shut his eyes hard, opened them, and forced himself to climb up to the top of a pile of oaken planks. But somewhere on the way up he realized that he was tired, very tired. Suddenly it was hard to pull the weight of his body. He couldn't remember when he had last eaten or slept. He couldn't remember when he had not been running and running, trying to get somewhere before it was too late.

I'd like to be where it's warm, he thought. And solid and still and where I wouldn't have to run. Lying in a field somewhere in the sun, near a river, with nowhere else to go. I could sleep there in the sun. . . .

The lumber was piled unevenly on top, so that Erik was able to squirm down into a kind of trough deep enough to shield him from the cold wind. He felt a little warmer, pressing down into the strong warm smell of the new lumber. When he raised his head a little to look around, the wind slashed his face with needles of rain. Shivering, he hugged the wet wood and peered down at the base of the pile of planks. It was less than twenty feet from the starboard rail. The area around the gangplank just below him was crowded with hundreds of whalemen. And then Erik saw the visitors' launch already pulling away. He stared after it, roaring away through the rising swells and flying scud until it disappeared in mist and spray.

Whalemen shouted above the wind. The general uproar of a factory ship getting under way filled the air. Men rushed about. The Tannoy bellowed, "Secure the hatches. . . .Check all storm lashings. . . ."

Boats still circled the ship as her giant turbines started vibrating through the deck plates. Erik tried to move. He tried to crawl over and down to the starboard gangplank, but he couldn't. He felt a kind of paralysis as he lay in the cleft of lumber away from the main force of the wind, gripping with numbing fingers one of the guy ropes that lashed down the stack of lumber.

The net of steel wires supporting the factory ship's cumbersome masts and stacks strummed and twanged in the wind. Smoke from the stacks billowed over the decks and over Erik and down across the rails and the surface of the fjord, which now resembled a greasy broth. Erik could barely see the piers. He glimpsed flashes of color in the mist: handkerchiefs, scarfs, skirts, umbrellas, all flooding together like dye in water. A moment later piers and hills and color and houses dissolved under the dark sky.

Erik flattened out hard on the planks. He buried his face in his folded arms. The smell of the wet oak was good, close to his nose, and suddenly a glad release flooded over him. A high excited pitch rang in his head, and he wanted to laugh. I'm this far, he thought.

Crewmen worked just below him, so close that Erik could have reached down and touched them. He thought of what Tiburon had said. If he could stay aboard until they were far enough down into the Southern Ocean, below South Georgia, he would be safe. They couldn't send him back then, not when they were deep into the frozen wilderness of the Scotia Sea. And once there, Bornak would have the power and authority to help him.

So I'll stay aboard somehow, he thought, without Bornak and Tiburon to help me find a hiding place and bring me food and water. He would have to stay completely out of sight—unheard, unseen, and unknown. As far as the *Arcturus* was concerned, he wouldn't even exist. He was a stowaway.

The sky darkened rapidly and the wind blew harder. Erik stayed where he was, hunched down as far as he could get out of the cold's freezing bite. He would wait until dark, he decided, when it would be safer to risk climbing down and looking for a better hiding place. His hands grew numb. Even the thoughts in his brain seemed to freeze. He kept his head down inside his collar, and his eyes closed, and for all he knew, he lay there for hours. The sound of the *Arcturus'* weighing anchor, the start of her ponderous swing down the Oslo Fjord, seemed unreal, far away. Other sounds faded in and out of his awareness like bits and pieces of memories—the bells ringing through the ship, the whistles from the bridge, whistles and sirens, foghorns and bells, sounding off from every ship and boat in the fjord.

Once he thought he heard Norway's national anthem, *Ja, vi elsker dette landet.*

Later he knew in a cold, real way that the *Arcturus* was steaming toward the North Sea and heading for the bottom of the world.

FOUR

When the *Arcturus* was well out into the darkness of the North Sea, Erik prowled through the shadows of the cargo deck, looking for a proper hiding place, one in which he might live safely during a long voyage.

He avoided areas too well lit by floodlights. When he saw the yellow oilskins of deckies gleaming in the light of their lanterns, he stayed low or crawled into some darker aisle.

He was sure that if he were caught anywhere north of the Scotia Sea and even if Bornak should plead his cause, Captain Haakonsson would show him no mercy. I'd be put ashore at the first port of call, Erik thought, or transferred to a passing freighter that agrees to haul excess baggage north to Norway.

No, he decided, I'd rather be dead than go back. He stopped wherever he was in the darkness and shivered. Yes, he thought emphatically, I swear I'd rather jump into the ocean than be sent back to jail or Uncle Grimstad's farm.

He thought uneasily a moment more about the oath. Then he shrugged. It was a sincere oath, he thought, but there was no point in being morbid. Right now he had to concentrate on finding a good hiding place. He needed a retreat where he could keep dry and warm, where he could sleep and eat and live for weeks.

The *Arcturus'* engines pulsed harder, and her pattern of roll became slower and wider as she sailed deeper into the dark swells of the North Atlantic.

A little later, icy weather forced Erik to abandon his search for the perfect place and duck into any sort of shelter at all. He settled for the first burrow he could scurry into, under a flapping wing of oily canvas. He crawled back through a narrow crevice between wooden crates. About twelve feet in, the opening widened enough so that he could lie down and stretch out comfortably.

After he laced the canvas opening securely with rope halyards, canvas all around and above shut out the wind and rain. Warmth from the heated compartments below seeped up through the deck plates. When Erik curled up in his sealskin coat and the blanket from his rucksack, he felt warm and dry. After a while he even felt cozy as he listened to the beat of the rain on the canvas and the whine of the wind that could not touch him.

He got flatbread and *geit ost* (goat cheese) out of his rucksack. He was ravenously hungry, but he ate only a few bites. Then the wind and the rain and the steady rhythmical roll of the ship had such a soothing effect that he went to sleep.

He slept a long time. He didn't know how long, and he didn't care. For several days he dozed off and woke up and ate and dozed off again. Sometimes he lay only partly awake in a happy, dreamlike stupor. When he moved at all, it was only to eat more flatbread and *geit ost* and to drink the rainwater he'd found he could catch in a loose pocket of the canvas.

He'd read about whalemen going mad during the long monotony of this haul to the Southern Ocean. Week after dragging week at a few hundred knots a day was supposed to drive men crazy. Erik had read about them. They got drunk and had bloody brawls. Sometimes they killed one another or themselves. So, he decided, it would be a fine idea to sleep all the way to the Scotia Sea.

Erik tried doing that. But after a few days he had exhausted his store of rainwater, and the air began to turn uncomfortably hot. He realized they were steaming toward the West Indies. They had to cross the Tropics to reach the freezing south.

The heat got worse and worse inside the cargo cave. Erik had to loosen the halyards lacing up the canvas. He had to get some ventilation. He also had to find more food and a supply of drinking water.

He had to risk sneaking out onto the open deck.

After dark he began prowling the moonlit alleyways. He found spigots that gave both fresh and salt water. He found empty bottles to store water in, and he found crates of rations from which he stocked his cave.

He bore the heat during the day and crept out at night to cool off. He kept slipping out and roaming on the cargo deck at night even after he had plenty of food and water stored. Gradually he came to realize that he was even hungrier for human companionship than he was for food.

Once he thought he heard Bornak calling to summon him from his cave. He started to crawl out into the sunlight, but there were no voices out there. The voices were inside his head. Another time he woke up hearing himself crying out with fear. Rats were running over his face, he thought. But he saw that he had only been dreaming and that the feel of rats was only that of his own sweat dripping off his face, down his neck and body.

Another time he imagined Bornak and Tiburon were sitting there with him. They were all good friends, laughing, joking, and playing cards. Bornak suddenly said they should go out onto the open deck, leave the hiding place. "Nothing to worry about now," Bornak told Erik. And Tiburon agreed, assuring Erik that it was now safe to walk around the deck during the day. "No one will bother you, kid. You're a prince of gunners," Bornak said. "You should be sitting on a throne by your harpoon gun, not hiding in here like a thief." Then Erik opened his eyes, shivering as though he had brain fever.

After that, he never spent another night alone in his cave.

He found all the company he needed, prowling the dark alleyways. Hundreds of whalemen had moved up onto the open decks to escape the heat below. They brought up canvas deck chairs; they put up hammocks and canvas shelters. They made tables of packing cases and gathered around the light from electric lanterns. They sang; they played guitars; and they played cutthroat bridge and told hair-raising tales of great hunts below the roaring forties.

Erik crawled so close to Shelty sailors, Scots engineers, flensers, lemmers, and Norskies that he felt a part of their company even though no one knew he was there. He learned to lie close to them all night, listening and watching.

He looked for the part of the deck where the harpoon gunners met, but he never found it.

He decided there probably was no such place on the cargo deck or anywhere in the lower deck areas. Harpoon gunners were like royalty. They were the aristocrats among whalemen. Too proud and mighty to have to associate with lesser breeds of men, they doubtless had a special deck of their own. It was probably somewhere up near the officers' quarters around the flying bridge.

Erik went back to his cargo cave and waited out the days.

The *Arcturus* anchored off Aruba in the West Indies and took on her full capacity of fuel oil: twenty thousand barrels. Soon after that Erik lay in his cave and listened to the ceremony that marked the crossing of the equator. Howls of mock fear went up as rookie seamen were baptized in tubs of salt water, then received certificates sealed with the Royal Order of Neptunis Rex.

A few days later Erik woke up and realized that the air was cold again. He shivered and risked a daylight look from his cave. An ominous gray horizon lay to the south, and the air seemed brittle as glass.

We must be at least south of the island of Tristan da Cunha, he thought. That meant they would soon anchor in the old whaling base of South Georgia Island. That will mean I've won, he exulted. He laughed softly, then stopped laughing as a quick icy gust cut at his face.

He had read about sudden and savage attacks of wind in the South Atlantic, Antarctic hurricanes that roared at ninety or more miles an hour off the five million square miles of the ice continent.

Reading about them had not prepared him for the actual assault. One moment there was hardly a sound as Erik looked uneasily through the slit in the canvas wall of his cave. The *Arcturus* rolled on in her steady, reassuring way. The next moment another sharp gust broke spray over the deck. Black storm clouds suddenly blanketed the sun. The sky fell to what seemed to be no more than six hundred feet, and soon the air turned into a wilderness of rain, spume, and choking spindrift.

All thirty thousand tons of the *Arcturus* yawed like a rowboat. Her turbines fought the giant press of waves and wind. Erik, hurled to his knees, clung to a guy rope as the sea sluiced the deck green to its length and flooded the confines of his hiding place.

Blinded, choking, he dug at the halyards that laced the canvas opening together. Tons of water poured in, and Erik knew that soon it would boil up over his head and choke him like a rat in a well.

FIVE

He scarcely remembered tearing loose the last halyard and being hurled out of his canvas cave by a roaring cataract. As the ship rolled to port, giant waves rushed over the cargo and made foaming rivers down the aisles. Erik felt himself swept helplessly along, spun, flipped end over end down the steeply slanted deck toward the railing and the waiting sea.

Waves curled forty feet above the ship. Erik kicked his legs. He threshed his arms, and he dug and clawed with his fingers against the merciless tons of water that slammed him down, flattened, smothered, choked, and hurled him into scraping timbers and rusted iron.

He grabbed at crate edges, wire cables, guy ropes, and splintering wood. But he was washed out of the cargo into the open alley of the scupperway between the cargo area and the thick, solid iron railing called the ship's bulwark. A wave started carrying him straight over the bulwark toward the deeps.

Just at that moment the ship floundered and rolled back again to starboard. Erik found himself washed back across the deck in a foot of water. Before he had time to get to his feet, the ship was rolling to port again. He scrabbled to the right toward a network of pipes very near the bulwark. He strained, rolled, squirmed, and kicked until he felt cold metal against his right hand. He clung there frantically trying to catch his breath.

Then he inched and dragged his weight across the pipes until he could get a firm grip with both hands and hold himself there against the force of the water.

The ship rolled back to starboard. This gave him a short respite. He got more breath back and a little more strength, enough to hook one leg through the pipes. Then he vomited salt water.

The ship rolled. It rolled again. Again and again the sea poured over him. He knew he was rapidly weakening and he was never able really to regain his breath. The waves came back too fast, and the cold sapped his energy and warmth away, turning his body numb.

Soon he realized most of the feeling had left his arms and hands. His fingers were starting to slip from their hold on the pipes. He admitted then that he had only one chance—one chance to save his life.

He squinted miserably at the door in the wall of the superstructure, less than twenty five feet away. Not far. Maybe he could make that run before another wave came back. His strength was almost gone, and the deck was slippery and steeply angled. But it was a short run, and he might just have time to make it to that door between the ship's rolls. He also had to open the door and get inside, or that next big wave would do him in.

He started to make his run. Then he saw the lifeboat. It hung from its davits, high and solid. He could get to it and climb the davits and be above the next wave quicker than he could cross the deck to the superstructure wall.

The lifeboat would be safe and warm under its canvas cover. Rations and plenty of water were undoubtedly stored inside. Once he was tucked away up there he wouldn't have to give himself up until they reached the Scotia Sea. He wondered why he had not thought of the lifeboat before. He leaped up and away from the pipes, and ran, ran in a final desperate burst, slipping, half-falling on the washed deck.

Bracing himself on the davits, above the rush of water now, he clung with his left hand to the line binding down the boat's cover. He dug his knife from his pocket with his right hand and cut the rope. He quickly knotted both severed ends to keep them from sliding through the eyeholes in the canvas. If the rope came loose, wind would whip the entire cover from the boat.

He now had three feet of rope loosened, enough so

that he could crawl under and inside. He sank down only partly conscious into the warm dry darkness.

He covered himself with blankets. When his shivering stopped, he opened a box of rations and ate. Then quickly he found a length of quarter-inch line and crawled back to the slit opening he'd left. It had to be laced up again without delay, before the wind got under and tore the canvas to shreds. Pushing his head and right arm through the opening into the screaming wind, he reached for one end of the severed rope.

He hesitated and looked down at the deck. He thought he heard in the wind a human cry. Waves battering the hull formed giant waterspouts fifty feet high. Erik kept looking and listening, and at first he saw nothing moving down there but the sea.

Then a man's body rolled out of a cargo aisle. It was almost beneath the lifeboat, bobbing into the scupperway like soggy driftwood. The receding sea would soon take the man over the side into the deep, but he was not struggling at all. His legs and arms flopped lifelessly as though he were unconscious.

Erik was already out of the lifeboat and dropping back down the davits to the deck. He stumbled in the wash and fell to his knees before the whipping wind. He struggled up again and lurched toward the helpless shape rolling toward the bulkhead. Almost blind again in freezing spume, he flung himself across the drowning man, got the quarter-inch line under him, around the bulging waist and tied in a Tarbuck knot that wouldn't slip and squeeze out whatever life the man had left in him.

He got the other end of the line through a ringbolt in the deck and wrapped the rope around his wrists just as the next wave buried him.

He came up strangling. Blindly he pulled the rope from the ringbolt and dragged the inert body along the remaining few feet of scupperway toward the door in the superstructure. With the line over his shoulder, he bent into the wind, heaving and hauling at the weight that hung behind him like lead.

Finally he touched the steel of the superstructure. He felt along, found the handle of the door, grabbed it, and sagged to his knees. He strained at the handle, hanging on it with all of his weight. But it stayed tight.

He dimly remembered pushing the loose end of the rope through the handle of the door and tying it about his own waist in another Tarbuck knot before another wave washed him over and beat him down.

The rope around his waist tore at him as if it would rip him in half. Another wave buried him. Another, and then another. He never knew how many. He lost count, and he seemed to be drowning in one long flood. But the rope held. The man on one end, Erik on the other end, anchored in the middle by the steel door handle, the rope held. . . .

A sour-faced medic told Erik that he'd been in sick bay, more or less unconscious, for fourteen hours. But only as a result of extreme exhaustion, overexposure, dehydration, poor diet, and seawater in the lungs. Otherwise nothing serious, the medic assured him. Erik was well on his way to recovery. The medic brought Erik a meal of roast whalemeat, cheese, and milk, with salt tablets for dessert.

"Didn't I swallow enough salt?" Erik asked.

"No," the medic said.

But all Erik really cared about was the ship. He knew from its lack of motion that the hurricane was past and that the *Arcturus* was at anchor. So they must have safely reached South Georgia Island!

That meant he was in under the wire. South Georgia was on the edge of the Scotia Sea. Captain Haakonsson, according to Tiburon, wouldn't consider sending him back now. It would be too difficult, too much of a waste of time and men and material. He checked with the medic, who was squinting at his clipboard and adjusting a pair of horn-rimmed glasses.

"Yes," the medic growled. "We're at South Georgia. The sinkhole of creation in my book. I never go topside unless I have to do it. But you're lucky to be here. You're lucky to be anywhere except feeding the sharks. And that's just where you'd be, sonny, if someone hadn't heard you kicking on the outside of that door."

"I don't remember doing that," Erik said, gulping

down more whalemeat. He put the tray back on the bedside table and drank the rest of the milk. I've made it, he thought. He wanted to jump up and dance around the room. Bornak would figure out a way to get Erik transferred to his whale catcher, and he'd soon be starting his gunner's apprenticeship.

Erik asked for his clothes.

"They're still in the ship's laundry," the medic said, startled. "What's the rush, sonny? The Old Man's sending you back north as soon as I give him your clean bill of health. I'd better give you one more quick checkup before—"

"Sending me back?" Erik whispered. He stared at the medic in disbelief. "Why would Captain Haakonsson waste money just to get me taken back to Montevideo? It doesn't make sense."

"You're lucky in spite of yourself," the medic said. "A Norwegian destroyer happens to be tied up here repairing her hull after running into an iceberg. The captain's agreed to drop you off on his way back to Montevideo. He'll be heading north in a few hours, after whale poachers who are shooting a lot of illegal whale northwest of Tristan da Cunha."

"It makes no sense at all!" Erik groaned. "I can work my way. I can earn a thousand times more in six months than it will cost to send me back."

"I said you were lucky," the medic said. "I don't know why you were stupid enough to stow away on this butcher ship. I'd rather think you were just mistaken and got on the wrong ship. Because you really don't look the least stupid, you know. Anyway, sonny, you're lucky you'll soon be heading north again toward civilization."

Erik sagged back in the bed and shook his head slowly. The medic stuck a thermometer in Erik's mouth and looked at his wristwatch. "Yes, sonny, you are lucky in spite of yourself. No matter what you've read in adventure stories, the Southern Ocean is a very bad place to spend the summer. Especially on a stinking butcher ship!"

He looked at the thermometer. "You'll live. I'll pass the word on to Captain Haakonsson. As I understand it, you'll be granted a hearing before the captain's review board. The verdict's a foregone conclusion, of course. You'll be sent back. But the Old Man's a stickler for regulations, so you have to be granted the token formality of a hearing before you're sent home."

Erik slid down into the bed and turned his face to the wall. The medic went out. A metal door clanged. Erik shut his eyes hard against the room, the ship, the world, and everything on it and around it—and that included the ancient whalemen's haven of South Georgia Island. None of it had anything any longer to do with him. The island was a speck in the South Atlantic, on the northern border of the Scotia Sea. It was a desolate place, swept by the world's most ferocious and freezing

45

winds. Yet it was also the most welcome of all harbors for voyage-weary whalemen eager to get whale. It was here the great hunt began.

But not for me, Erik thought, and the full sickening impact of his defeat shivered through him like a feverish chill. Tears burned in his eyes; he wiped at them fiercely. He wasn't feeling sorry for himself. He was beaten that was all, and he might as well face it. Anyway, he reminded himself awhile later, I'm alive.

He laughed a little then at that silly oath of his—to think that he'd sworn to jump into the sea rather than to give himself up. He'd rather go anyplace now than into the sea, he thought—even back to Uncle Grimstad.

He wondered why Bornak didn't try to help him now. He reminded himself that Bornak might not even know he had managed to stay aboard the *Arcturus*. Even if Bornak had heard about the stowaway in sick bay, he would have no way of knowing the stowaway was Erik Nordahl, alias Orm Gudmundsen. Still he should be able to make a good guess. Maybe something had happened, and Bornak couldn't help him now.

His laundered clothes were soon brought in by another medic who told Erik to put them on, double quick, and report at once to the Captain's quarters for his hearing before the review board.

A bosun with a sharktooth ring in his left ear conducted Erik to the Captain's cabin under the flying bridge.

SIX

Erik stood at rigid and puzzled attention. The captain's review board was an odd one. It consisted only of the captain.

The captain was small, brown, and bald, a weathered old seadog who sat bent over a table covered with oceanic charts and maps. His quarters reminded Erik of a millionaire's study, with its red carpets, drapes, chairs of sea-elephant hide stretched on mahogany frames, expensive whalebone carvings, a central chandelier made of four seal skulls expertly matched.

There's a lot of money in whaling, Erik thought. Gunners were supposed to get rich, too, shooting whales. But Erik's father had never seemed to have much money. He wondered why for a moment, then reminded himself that it no longer mattered.

"Feel well enough to travel?" Captain Haakonsson said.

"Yes—yes, sir."

"Name?" He peered at Erik with tired, washed-out eyes.

"Er—Orm Gudmundsen." Erik blurted out the false name Tiburon had told him to use, although he wondered bitterly if it mattered now what name he used—or if he had a name at all.

"Home?"

"Lopphavet, sir."

"Lopphavet? That's in Norway?"

"Up north, sir."

"Must be in Lapland."

"No, sir."

"Don't be impertinent."

"No, sir."

"Parents?"

"No parents, sir."

"Age?"

"Eighteen, sir."

"Proof of these statements?"

"No, sir. Lost everything, sir, in the hurricane."

"Including your life almost. I'll give you this, mister. You showed heart trying to rescue that poor devil of a blubberboy. But it's no excuse for being a shark-brained stowaway. Is it now?"

"No, sir."

"Why in holy name would you want to stow away on this floating butchery, lad? I can understand a young man wanting to run away to sea. Did it myself. But—see here. Did you ever butcher animals?"

"Why—no. No, sir—"

"Don't those land crabs around Lopphavet still do their own butchering. Pigs, cows, sheep?"

"Er—yes, sir. But I—I never did it, sir."

"Ever work around a slaughter house?"

"No—I—I never did, sir."

"Well, this ship's a slaughter house that floats. That's all. It's a factory for butchering and processing whale meat into oil and other things, including cat food. But think, if you can, of butchering a cow weighing as much as fifty elephants! A cow that leaks twenty-three thousand tons of blood, whose tongue weighs nine thousand pounds. This is a far bigger slaughterhouse than any you might find in Norway, but it's a slaughterhouse just the same. You would have saved yourself time and trouble, and made more money, if you'd gone into the butcher business at home."

"I—didn't want to be a meat cutter, sir. I wanted to go whaling. I decided to take my chances rather than stay at home and be a land crab the rest of my life."

"But a stowaway!" Captain Haakonsson frowned. "That's the lowest thing there is at sea, lower than a rat or a cockroach."

"I know, sir. I didn't intend to be a stowaway, sir. Not at first. I came aboard hoping to stay on as a deckie or something. But I got lost in the cargo. The storm came up. I—I just couldn't seem to get back ashore, sir."

Captain Haakonsson nodded with rough understanding and sympathy. "Well, we're skipping your hearing for now, lad. Your brave act during the hurricane won you some powerful friends in this fleet. Among them is Bornak, the king of gunners. He asked me to grant you a stay of execution, so to speak. So have several other gunners and whalemen."

Suddenly Erik's knees felt a bit unsteady.

"Gunners go out and hunt and shoot the whale," Captain Haakonsson said wryly. "Without whale, none of us would get oil. If we don't get oil, we get no money, and we go home broke. So gunners are very influential people out here. If Bornak and his gunners suggest that I do you a special favor, why I have to consider doing that favor. Understand?"

"Ye—yes, sir."

"If they suggest that I give a brave young stowaway a special break, I consider it. I don't have to do it. I'm still the captain, understand? The captain! Even though the company now calls me a mere manager, I'm the captain." The old man sniffed defiantly. "I do not have to take orders from gunner captains, not even from Bornak. But I have agreed to give you a break, lad. I must do it legally, according to the laws of the sea. Everything here must be legal, or I never would do it, you understand. It must be by the book!"

"Yes, sir," Erik whispered.

"Maritime law says that a stowaway can be put to work if it's necessary to fill a crew vacancy, a vital crew shortage. A regular crewman may be injured or killed, go overboard. If a stowaway happens to be around, he can be made to fill the missing seaman's shoes. That's the law."

He leaned toward Erik. His pale eyes narrowed. "So I will keep you aboard, mister, because Bornak and his gunners ask it, and because it's legal. You will fill the shoes of the dead man."

"De—dead man," Erik whispered hoarsely.

"Yes, the man whose life you tried to save."

"Dead?"

"Aye, the blubberboy was dead before you even rescued his remains. Or so the medical officer tells me. You nearly lost your life trying to save one that was already lost. Anyway you'll take his place on the blubber decks. And that's how it'll be legal."

"Blubber decks!" The words strangled in his throat. He coughed.

"On the aft flensing deck, mister. That's where they rip the blubber off the whale. You'll have the same job as the man whose life you tried to save. He was a blubberboy, so that makes you a blubberboy. Right, mister?"

Erik's hands trembled at his sides. He clenched his fists in an effort to control his humiliation and outrage. Blubberboys were the absolute bottom scum of the Southern Ocean. For a prince of gunners, no job could be more degrading.

But, he amended his thoughts quickly, I'm supposed

to be Orm Gudmundsen. Orm Gudmundsen, ignorant mountain oaf, would be grateful for the chance to serve as blubberboy. He wouldn't be proud. He wouldn't think being a blubberboy was a shameful disgrace.

So Erik bowed a little and shuffled his boots. "Thank you, sir," he said, trying to sound pleased and humble; and maybe he was a little bit. He was staying with the fleet. He still had a chance. Bornak knew he was here and was helping him stay.

"Now hear this, mister!" warned the captain. "You're on strict probation. All that matters on a factory ship is oil! Oil and more oil. So you work on that blubber deck, mister, like a demon, or else. You'll be on trial here, mister. Show a strong back, move faster than a school of hungry shark, and I'll keep you aboard. Fall down on the job, and I'll put you ashore on South Georgia and let you rot there until someone feels like taking you home. You get that, mister?"

"Yes, sir," Erik said faintly. "Thank you, sir."

"Report to the flensing deck aft, to chief flenser Skaug. If you can't find him look for Old Kra in the blubber hold."

Erik thanked Captain Haakonsson again and took his leave.

As Erik stepped out onto the open deck, an icy wind seemed to freeze the sweat on his face. He stood there awed by his first look at the Antarctic.

52

A strange sort of sun, small and dark red, shone from a greenish sky. Ice refracted shafts of light in dazzling spectrum. Black, ice-streaked mountains soared straight up for thousands of feet around Stromness Bay in which the *Arcturus* lay at anchor. This last unexplored corner of the world seemed to promise adventures of some weird and unpredictable kind.

He took deep breaths of the freezing air and looked aft down the acres of cargo deck. Much of the cargo was cleared away now. The rest was going below or over the side onto waiting whale-catcher boats.

Erik worked his way back cautiously along the port scupperway, through a tangle of working machines and men.

He caught his breath as he saw the rest of the big, deadly-looking whale catchers steaming toward the *Arcturus* and tying up alongside. When the *Arcturus* went back to Norway at the end of the season, these nine boats always remained behind. Here in Stromness Bay, protected from hurricane winds, the catchers waited at anchorage for the return of the mother ship. Like a pack of chained wolves they waited for the mother ship to come back and release them for the hunt. Now set free, they raced across the bay, raging and chafing to get out into the ice floes and kill.

One by one the boats tied up alongside the *Arcturus* to take on fuel, men, and materials for the hunt. Deck winches swung nets of cargo over onto a black-steeled, five-hundred-ton catcher tied up less than fifty feet from Erik.

As each section of the *Arcturus'* deck was cleared, carpenters descended on it with hammers and power saws. They quickly converted piles of lumber into an oaken platform that would soon cover the whole deck, turning it into a gigantic butcher's block.

Shelty workcrews shouted orders around Erik. They trundled barrels and crates around him. They spliced wire cables, overhauled steering gear, packed winch glands, opened hatches, geared up derricks and steam winches and freed crutch lashings. But Erik hardly heard them, or saw anything else but the whale catcher just on the other side of the starboard bulwark. He stood, frozen with awe and longing, looking at the catcher's high, flared bow and at the name newly painted there in bright red: WHALE CATCHER ONE.

Whale Catcher One, Erik thought. Bornak's catcher.

Men were directing the loading of *Catcher One*, but Erik saw no sign of Bornak or Tiburon. Only the boat; it was eighty feet long, five hundred tons, very low in the stern with a high midships superstructure and smokestack. At the top of its tall mast was the swaying lookout barrel.

Erik's gaze went back to the bow. He stared, transfixed, at the black iron base on which was mounted the harpoon gun. A protective canvas hood covered the gun but not its brutal, thick-barreled outline.

Erik imagined himself standing there behind it, sighting down that barrel at the back of a big blue. So near, he kept thinking. So near—a jump and a few steps, and he would be there where a prince of gunners belonged.

"Orphan boy," a familiar voice said just behind him. "You're a long way from Lopphavet."

Erik turned. Tiburon studied him curiously. His grin was somewhat friendly. "Congratulations. You're doing all right for a land crab."

"Sure," Erik said. "A scummy blubberboy!"

Tiburon shrugged. "Cheer up. You're still on board, my boy, and the worst is yet to come."

"Worse? What could be worse than being a measly blubberboy? Why can't Bornak take me aboard his catcher now? I want to shoot whale!"

"Patience. You'll find out. Bornak'll have you killing whales as soon as he can manage."

"Until then couldn't Bornak arrange something a little more suitable for a brother gunner?" Erik grumbled. "Say, a bilge swab? Or a mop jockey?"

"You're lucky to be here at all," Tiburon said, "instead of on your way back to Uncle Grimstad's farm. I don't know why Bornak bothers with you."

"I wonder about that myself," Erik said. "This is some way to serve my gunner's apprenticeship, dragging blubber around."

"Why didn't you get in touch with Bornak when you came aboard like you were supposed to do?"

"If I could have seen Bornak, I would have," Erik said. "I did the best I could."

"Well, getting you assigned to the butcher deck was the best Bornak could do for you, too. At least, for now."

"How long do I have to drag blubber?"

"Bornak said to tell you he'll get you onto *Catcher One* as soon as he can after the whale killing starts. But whatever happens you've got to be patient and trust Bornak."

"That's all he said?"

"No. He also said it's still very important for you to be Orm Gudmundsen. Forget Erik Nordahl. You wouldn't know Erik Nordahl if you met him face to face. Those are Bornak's strict orders."

"Why?" Erik asked.

"I don't know why."

"When is as soon as he can?" Erik asked. "Look here, Tiburon. I'm grateful to Bornak for the chance to stay with the fleet. All right, I can take the blubber deck for a while. But for how long? I ought to have some idea of how long?"

Tiburon hesitated. "As soon as he can—that's all Bornak said. But when Bornak will get you transferred to his catcher isn't what you should be worrying about, kid."

"What should I be worrying about?"

"Whether you can stick to the job on the butcher

deck is what you should be worrying about. The blubber deck may be the scummiest job in the fleet, but it's also the toughest. You be careful, or you won't even live long enough to be transferred to *Catcher One*."

"Thanks," Erik said. "It's good to get a word of encouragement."

"Any time," Tiburon said. His thin mocking grin came back. "Just haul that blubber and wait and be patient."

Tiburon walked on along the bulwark toward the catcher. Erik didn't watch him go. He didn't want to look at *Catcher One* any more right now. He couldn't understand why Bornak couldn't take him aboard the catcher. Why should he have to be a measly blubber scum?

He walked on aft. As soon as he reached the flensing deck, he sensed trouble.

SEVEN

Erik felt the pinching cold on the back of his neck. Ten thousand feet up glittered the cone of a glacier with a rag of cloud hanging motionless around its peak. Scores of penguins and seals called out plaintively from the bay-shore rocks. Over everything was that curious and ominous smell of frozenness that only the Antarctic can produce.

Erik stood uneasily near the wall of the aft superstructure. Six men sat with their backs against it. Erik stood in front of them, but the men said nothing to him or to one another. They were sharpening and oiling their flensing knives.

"I'm supposed to report to the head flenser," Erik said. The flensers didn't look up. Erik gulped. He had never seen these knives before or been especially interested in them. As one destined to be a king of gunners, he had never dreamed he would end up working anywhere on a factory ship. All he knew about flensing knives was that they were used to strip the blubber from whale carcasses. Now he saw that they were ugly, curved, scimitarlike blades on the ends of four-foot-long handles. When a redbearded flenser pulled a hair from his beard and touched it to his blade, the hair parted and drifted off through the sunlight like two tiny insects.

Redbeard chuckled. He spun the knife and flipped it from one hand to the other. He seemed to notice Erik for the first time. "Yah?" he said.

"I was told to report to the flensing deck."

"You'd be the stowaway."

"Yes, sir."

"Cap'n sent word he was sending us a blubberboy." The other flensers blinked up at Erik curiously. Redbeard stood up, twirling his blade like a baton. "Well, stowaway. Nobody's privileged to speak to Skaug the chief flenser until the first whale's killed. That's the rule. In any case, Skaug never stoops to talk to blubber scum."

Erik felt the back of his neck burn with humiliation. Hold on now, he warned himself. You're on strict probation. Don't be proud and don't lose your temper. Just be Orm Gudmundsen, clumsy mountain oaf.

He hunched his shoulders and ducked his head and hoped that he looked shyly ignorant and utterly harmless. He managed to stammer a little, too: "I just know the Cap'n said to report here."

Redbeard pointed his knife at a partly opened manhole in the deck. "Yah, you got to report down there to Old Kra. He's head of the blubberboys."

Erik started to move toward the manhole but stopped very suddenly when Redbeard's knife flashed out. It clipped off the top button of Erik's coat and the button flea-hopped across the deck planks. "Just hold on, boy," Redbeard said. "We have to test you out to see if you qualify as a blubberboy. You don't think just anybody can come down here and be a blubberboy, do you?"

"No, sir."

"Stand over there against the bulwark."

Erik moved back until his legs touched cold steel. Behind him he heard the lap and chuckle of waves against the *Arcturus'* hull. Redbeard walked to the hatch leading down into the blubberboys' hold. He kicked it open and yelled down. "Your stowaway's here."

Redbeard jumped aside, and a dozen or so unkempt and ragged men of all types and ages spilled out across the deck. Each man skillfully swung by a wooden handle an ugly, heavy iron hook. The hook was over two feet long with a point as shiny and sharp as the barb on a giant fishhook. Each blubberboy seemed to regard his hook as an extension of his arm. He motioned with it, pointed with it, leaned on it to steady himself against the ship's roll.

Two rows of men quickly formed a lane: flensers on one side, twirling knives; blubberboys on the other side, flashing their hooks.

Most of the crewmen working on the decks stopped to gather about and watch. Officers looked down from the flying bridge.

"Run," Redbeard shouted suddenly. "If you can run through to the far end of this gauntlet, you'll be worthy of the name of blubberboy."

Erik licked his lips slowly and tried to ease the tension knotting his stomach. He had endured initiation in boarding school. He had run the gauntlet and stood up to the lines of clubs and belts. The pain was far easier to take than the injury to his pride. But a gauntlet of belts and clubs was one thing; hooks and knives were quite another. This time he forgot his pride and thought only about the physical pain and the chance of serious injury to life and limb.

He tried to grin, but his lips would not obey. Instead he felt his lower lip quivering.

"Run," Redbeard said. "Run for your life."

Erik suddenly felt the sweat seeping down his face. He wiped his forehead and eyes on his coat sleeve and lunged away from the bulwark. He ran straight for Redbeard, the first man in the line.

The knives and hooks whirred and clicked like the metallic wings and mandibles of giant beetles. He faltered. His knees quivered, but he forced himself on.

Redbeard was suddenly there before him. "Jump," he shouted. "Jump for your life, stowaway." And he swung his flensing knife at Erik's knees.

Without breaking stride, Erik jumped. He swung his arms as if they were wings to gain height, and he pumped his knees up to his chin. He wasted no time in looking down to see if he had cleared the blade. While still in the air, he was looking ahead, judging how best to avoid the next blade, the next hook, then a forest of whirring blades and hooks.

He ran; he leaped; he twisted; he dodged and flinched and ducked. He hopped and swerved and kept on running. He mustn't stop. And the only way to go was straight ahead. . . .

Something thudded on the top of his head as if he had hit a concrete wall. Light exploded before his eyes, and pain stabbed down the length of his body and buckled his knees. His outflung arms and the flats of his hands smacked against the deck plates. But he forced himself onto his hands and knees at once. He kept moving ahead, crawling, until he found strength enough to push himself to his feet. Then he was up and running again.

Plunging blindly now, gritting his teeth, he hardly knew when he jumped or how, but only that he must keep going.

Another hook slashed out at him; he dodged it. Another blade swung, and he ducked. He seemed to be running on and on, avoiding knives and hooks, but never getting anywhere, as if he were on a treadmill. He couldn't see the end of the gauntlet now. Maybe it had no end.

Air burned in his lungs. A blow glanced off the side of his head, and he fell to one knee. He struggled hard this time to get up again, and when he ran on, he felt fire crackling across the backs of his legs. Everything, knives, hooks, and faces were fading and turning fuzzy. Once he put his hand to his mouth to stop a yell of pain. He fell again, and then again, and each time he was knocked down, he took longer to struggle back to his feet.

He managed to stay on his feet, but the strength to jump finally failed him. His legs suddenly buckled under him. He lay there then, somewhere, with his face pressed against the deck. Maybe I can't get up anymore, he thought.

He twisted his head, got one eye open, and saw blurred faces and blades moving in a strange way. They seemed to move in slow motion, fading in and out of view. He shut his eyes hard and forced his mind to a desperate clarity. The gauntlet was never very long, he reminded himself. It had never been longer than halfway across the deck. After all his running and jumping he knew he ought to be near the end of it, whether he could see the end or not.

So I really should keep going, he decided. No one had made a strict rule that he had to run and jump all the way to the end. Any method might be permissible as long as he kept moving.

Maybe they would allow me to crawl, he thought. Why not? He couldn't seem to get back up onto his feet, and he might as well try crawling if that was the only way he could move.

He slid one hand forward, then a knee. He braced that hand and knee firmly, then carefully slid forward the other hand, the other knee. He repeated the process. It seemed a little easier the third time, and he was encouraged to keep going. He had not crawled since he was a baby. Evidently it was like swimming; once you learned it, you never quite forgot how it was done. And crawling was better than running. He did not have to worry about falling down.

A blade hung in front of his face. With a long heavy effort he lifted his hand and pushed the blade to one side.

Later—much later it seemed to Erik—he stopped crawling. He couldn't remember exactly when he stopped. All he knew was that suddenly he was just lying there somewhere on the deck, flat on his stomach, his face on one folded arm. He lay there awhile, taking long gasping breaths. Then he turned his head carefully and blinked one eye toward the light.

He realized then that there was no more reason to crawl, no reason to move at all. There were no more men waiting, no more hooks, no more knives.

Then he was surprised to find himself not running or jumping or crawling—but flying. No, he couldn't be flying. It was the mob of blubberboys. They had hoisted him up onto their shoulders, and they were carrying him toward the blubberboys' hold. They were carrying him above their heads, and they were cheering him and shouting congratulations as though he were some sort of hero. Hurrah, hurrah for Orm Gudmundsen, the blubberboy!

Well, Erik thought as he grinned up at the sky, I always have dreamed of being a hero. . . .

EIGHT

When Erik opened his eyes, he was lying below on a greasy mattress. The overhead bunk was about twelve inches from his nose. A swollen bruise behind his right ear throbbed with pain. He felt better when he discovered he had no broken bones. His head, though, and his back ached and burned.

Erik wrinkled his nose. The blubberboys' hold was an undersized rat's nest, a tangle of greasy clothing, tables, crates, bottles, blubberhooks, and scraps of uneaten food. A few draggly shapes snored from the deck or on bunks. Others sat at makeshift tables playing cards.

The air was thick, foul, like vapor from a vat of stale soup. The smell of unwashed bodies and gear was mixed with another kind of stench that had seeped down for years from the overhead butcher decks. It had dribbled down into every dark crack and cranny of the ship, away from the reach of cleaning swabs and sunlight— the cod-liver smell of dead whales.

Well, Erik thought as he went back to sleep, it's a small price to pay for membership in the Royal Order of Blubberboys.

He was shaken awake by an old man whose ragged sweater hung on him as though he were a bag of bones. "Welcome," he croaked, "to the blubber deck, Orm Gudmundsen. I'm head blubberboy, Old Kra."

Erik shook a gnarled, dry hand, scaled like a big bird's claw, and knew why they had given him the name of Old Kra. Old Kra swung a whale hook with his left hand when he talked to emphasize his words. "I can't teach you much about blubbering, Orm. You'll just have to wait and learn as you go."

Erik nodded. He nodded again when Old Kra told him to rest up, and when he was rested to check out some cold-weather gear. He would sign a chit for whatever he drew, and at the voyage's end the amount would be taken out of his pay.

"All right, Old Kra, sir," Erik said. He would need the clothes, but the rest of Old Kra's advice didn't concern him. He didn't intend to be on the butcher decks long enough to worry about getting blubberboy's pay at the season's end. In a very short time he'd be out there with Bornak on the bow of *Whale Catcher One*. He would be sighting down the barrel of the harpoon gun at the back of a running blue. He would be drawing apprentice gunner's pay, plus a fat bonus for every whale killed by *Catcher One*. Erik knew, though, that if he ever got behind a harpoon gun and was hunting the great whale he wouldn't care about the money. The hunt itself would be pay enough.

Erik jumped, startled, as Old Kra slammed another whale hook into the wood of the bunk frame just above Erik's head. Erik stared at it quivering there a few inches away. He slowly licked his lips.

"Practice with your whale hook, lad," Old Kra warned. "Practice until you handle that hook the same as you handle your right arm."

He pointed at a blubberboy in an adjoining bunk. The fellow was asleep, but his right hand was raised above his head, still firmly gripping the handle of his whalehook. "A blubberboy even sleeps with his hook ready," Old Kra said. "As soon as you rest, start practicing. Swing and balance, hone your hook and sharpen your aim. A real blubberboy can do anything with his hook. That goes for eating and darning his socks."

Erik vowed to practice hard. He might not be on the butcher deck more than a week or two, but while he was there, he had to give a good account of himself. Captain Haakonsson had put him on strict probation. If he wasn't a competent blubberboy, he might still be exiled to South Georgia Island for the rest of the season.

He thanked Old Kra and went back to sleep. . . .

He slept for almost twenty-four hours. After that he lay partly awake, listening to the unceasing clang and click of whale hooks being cleaned, sharpened, and swung in practice.

The blubberboys were a sullen lot. When they did talk, they talked only about whales and whale oil.

"Those hunters had better do a lot more killing than last year, or we'll never reach our oil quota," someone grumbled.

"Gunther says we'll never make our quota this season. We'll go home broke, and our families will all have to live on government welfare. That's what Gunther says."

"Gunther could be right."

"He'd better not be right. We've got to hit that quota!"

"That's right!"

"How can hunters kill more whale than last year when they've overkilled?"

"You really think they've overkilled?"

"Didn't the hunters have a hard time finding whale last season—especially big blues?"

"Sure they've overkilled," someone shouted bitterly. "They've slaughtered illegal whale all over, in every ocean of the world, until there's not enough left to go around."

"That's hard to believe. Why there were millions and millions of big whales in the Antarctic seas and—"

"—and millions of them have been slaughtered," interrupted the bitter voice. "Illegal whale, mother whales, young whales, all of them murdered by greedy fools, until now they're almost wiped out. Hundreds of steel catchers have butchered everything that swims with cannons and bombs! Now we're paying for stupid greed!"

"But Bornak's promised to find us plenty of big blues this time."

"That's right; that's right! Bornak's promised a big haul. We'll make our quota."

"Bornak, Bornak!" shouted the bitter voice. "He promises us enough big blue whale to make us all rich men. But if Bornak knows where to find all those blues, why didn't he find any blues last year?"

"Yes, yes. What about last season?"

"He couldn't even find ten blues last year when we needed the oil!"

And they went on and on while Erik dozed off and woke up and dozed again. It was the first he'd heard about any really serious shortage of whale. Conservationists had always warned against the indiscriminate slaughter of whale. The International Whaling Commission at Sandefjord was concerned about saving the whale from possible extinction. The commission had made conservation laws and sent out whaling inspectors to try to enforce them.

But Erik knew that whalemen had always laughed at these whaling laws and scoffed at the idea that the world's oceans would ever run out of whale. "There'll always be whale!" was their cry.

Erik wouldn't worry about it now, he decided. He was sure that Bornak would never have promised the men a great haul of blues—enough to make everyone rich—unless he knew he could fulfill the promise.

Bornak will find those blues, Erik thought. Bornak will find and kill plenty of other whales, too, including big finbacks. And I'll be out there on the gundeck of *Catcher One* helping him do it. It was a pleasant thought to go back to sleep with, and Erik's dreams were rich with big blue whales.

South was the order. South steamed the *Arcturus* with her fleet of corvettes, buoy boats, and whale catchers. They sailed away from South Georgia into the freezing desolation of the Scotia Sea. The last human habitation fell behind. Now, for six months, the entire fleet ot ships and seven hundred men would disappear into a wilderness of fierce winds, sea, and pack ice—those vast masses of sea ice formed by the crushing together of pans, floes, and brash.

Erik wanted to go topside and get at least a look at South Georgia as they sailed away. But Old Kra stopped him with the words, "No one goes up there, lad, until the first whales are brought in to the knives."

Erik gave Old Kra no argument. He sat in the hold and sharpened his hook. He knew he had to be a good boy and obey orders.

The *Arcturus* was steaming across the Scotia Sea into the big whaling grounds, the great freezing seas that border the Antarctic ice-continent. Bornak as leader of the gunner captains, and of the nine catchers, was taking *Catcher One* far out ahead of the others. He was scouting for especially big pods of whale, and when he spotted them, he would report their positions to the *Arcturus*. He would send the report in by secret code via radio-telephone so that other competing fleets would be unable to reach the whale pods first.

But a long week passed with no whale sightings. A few days later some small whale pods were found by cruising gunners. But they were illegal whales, Old Kra said. They were female with calves, diseased whales, or they were too small. Such whales, according to the laws of the whaling commission, were not supposed to be taken. "That's why it's getting harder to find whale," Old Kra said, "and why they say the whale may become extinct. The men kill too many females and young ones. The animals are killed faster than they can reproduce."

The blubberboys shook their fists at the top decks and the offices of the whaling inspectors.

"Bring us whale!" was the angry cry. "We want whale!"

Erik joined the cry. The sooner whale started coming in, he hoped, the sooner Bornak would have him transferred to *Catcher One*. He sharpened his hook. He practiced whirling it about. He waited with the others for whale to come in to the butcher decks. All the time he dreamed of the moment when he would step onto the gun deck of *Catcher One* and be given his first chance behind the harpoon gun.

Then it came. The ship's siren blasted out the eagerly

awaited signal that the gunners had hit. Corvettes were hauling whales in to the butcher decks. Soon oil, precious oil, would be filling the storage tanks.

Erik found himself shouting wildly and running with the other blubberboys up and out into the biting cold of the flensing deck. With them, he swung his hook and danced to keep warm. The brittle wind seemed to cut straight into his bones. Men rushed about starting up winch motors. They cleared cables, opened cooker holes in the deck, started power-driven slicing machines and bone saws. Steam engines clattered, and cables snapped and whined above the deck.

Old Kra whooped with joy. He hopped about, a tattered old Army topcoat flapping around his bones. "Big whale pod coming in. Plenty of fat whale, boys!"

Erik looked off starboard through the pale polar sunlight. He saw a fast corvette steaming in toward the stern of the factory ship. It was dragging six huge carcasses that Erik immediately and proudly recognized as two fin whales, a sei, and three small humpbacks. Their cavernous mouths were hanging open, and this would cause too heavy a drag if they were towed headfirst. So they were hooked to the corvette's bows by their tails, three on a side, bellies turned up, shining white and flaccid. Above the corvette circled clouds of hungry, screaming seabirds.

Erik saw huge ice islands less than a mile away—icebergs, several miles long and three or four hundred feet high, drifting out of the mist. They were strangely shaped, like castles and fortresses, and they gleamed in the sunlight with a bluish-green fire. They had broken off from the edge of the Antarctic ice continent, and they were now drifting north into thousands of miles of warming and empty seas toward Cape Town.

". . . just hook that blubber and don't stop for anything," Old Kra was advising Erik solemnly. "Don't ever fall behind, lad. Don't let blubber pile up. If that happens, we're all in deep trouble."

"What'll happen then?"

"The flensers will rub your face in the blubber," Old Kra said. "If they ever do that to you once, lad, you'll never want it done again. There's only one big sin on this ship—and that's holding up production, losing a few barrels of oil."

Erik nodded and waited, and then Old Kra had another warning: "It's always heads up, or you'll get yours knocked off, lad. Deadly things fly through the air here. Watch sharp for flying shackles, knives, hooks, blubber, broken saw blades and cables. And watch out for the cooker holes. Boiling vats of oil down there. One slip, and you're just a bubble of grease."

A moment later Old Kra's mouth quivered. "There, the slipway's opening," he croaked. "Get ready, Orm. They'll be dragging them up to the knives!"

NINE

Steel mesh gates slid apart. The opening in the superstructure wall was twelve feet wide and twelve feet high, its bottom flush with the deck. Erik edged over for a closer look and peered down the slanted length of a long steel tunnel. It angled through the ship's center, from the flensing deck to the waterline. Staring into the dripping gloom, Erik saw dead whales bobbing about at the bottom of the tunnel.

A thick cable snaked past Erik. It slid down the slipway floor, preceded by a gigantic iron-jawed head. This was the *hval kra*, a huge hook, or whale clawer. As it grated down the incline, it opened its rusted jaws that were bigger than boxcars.

Men shouted signals up and down the tunnel, directing the *hval kra* until it made the proper connection with a whale's tail. Then the jaws snapped shut on the tail with a tremendous clang.

A steam winch howled behind Erik as the terrible strain was put on the cable. The machine sang and trembled as it dragged the *hval kra* back up the slipway. The colossal whale filled the tunnel as it slid up the incline. Tons of water and blood sloshed down from it. Seabirds flew out ahead of the whale and turned screaming above the decks. Then the smell hit Erik like a physical blow.

Gagging, he stumbled back, tripped, and almost fell. It was so much worse than anything Erik had ever smelled before that it seemed indescribable, overwhelming, acrid, stifling, and thick as gravy.

Old Kra steadied him. "It's happened to all whalers, lad. Ninety tons of dead flesh in the water more than thirty hours. That's bad. But you'll get used to it."

The flensers waited in two rows on either side of the slipway opening. Old Kra and the blubberboys stood farther back toward the center deck, between the cooker holes and the steam-driven slicing blades.

The twelve-foot flukes of the whale flopped from the opening. The body swelled out onto the deck between the rows of waiting flensers. A welcoming roar went up: "Skaug! Skaug!"

Skaug, the chief flenser, who never left his private quarters until the first whale moved up the slipway, now appeared. He leaped suddenly through an opening in the superstructure like a bird of prey. Tall, gaunt, all in black, he waved his gleaming knife. He jumped to the side of the whale before it was halfway out of the slipway opening. He plunged the curved blade of his knife into the flesh wall of the whale. Standing firm, legs braced, he held the knife there and let the winch do the work of drawing the flesh past him while he made a long precision cut in the blubber.

Then the other flensers rushed in, slashing at the blubber. Meanwhile, the whale was being hauled on out, free of the slipway, along the deck. Skaug, with quick skill, hacked steps into the wall of blubber and ran up them to the top of the whale. There he stood balancing on the finner's belly, his spiked boots digging into the flesh, his hooked knife raised above his head like a talon. The blade plunged down and buried itself to the haft. The whale sagged, blew a cloud of pink froth. And that overwhelming smell hit Erik again. It was worse, if possible, than before, like a poisonous vapor. It drove Erik backward, gagging and choking.

"Heads up, you stupid snipe!" The warning jerked Erik around. He'd nearly backed into the whirring blades of a slicer.

Another shout spun him back around. A frightful sound rent the air as if thousands of yards of heaving sailcloth were tearing in a hurricane wind. The flensers were making long cuts through the six-inch coat of blubber. Winch cables, attached with toggles, were pulling the blubber from the carcass in great blankets that swung dripping across the deck at express-train speed.

Skimming the heads of blubberboys, the blubber was dropped near the knives.

Steam-driven slicers tore into the blubber and piled up chunks small enough to be pushed down through the round cooker holes in the deck.

"Jump to, jump to, you blubberboys!" shouted Old Kra.

Erik ran in behind several others, so he could see what they did. They leaped. They hopped under the cables like a gathering of Captain Hooks out of a bad dream. They whammed their hooks into chunks of sliced blubber, slid them free of the pile, swung them about, and guided them skillfully and at great speed across the deck to the cooker holes that were now belching clouds of hot steam.

Erik slapped his hook home, dragged a chunk of oozing blubber from the pile, and eased it across the slippery deck.

"Faster," said Old Kra.

Erik tugged harder, sweat bursting from his face. He got the blubber near a cooker hole, disengaged his hook, and kicked the mound of fat down into the steam. He drew back, half falling as hundreds of tiny bubbles of scalding grease speckled his face.

"Faster now, faster, lad!" shouted Old Kra.

Erik stumbled back to the blubber pile.

The whales kept coming up the slipway. The blubber

blankets kept soaring through the air. Erik tried to go faster, but the blubber piled up.

Whenever he paused, hoping to stretch a little and catch his breath, Old Kra or someone else shouted, "Faster, faster!"

Once, through the steam, Erik saw an odd little man also running fast. Later he saw him again. Then he realized that every time another whale came up the slipway, there was the hurrying little man, always carrying a black notebook and a measuring tape of the kind used by surveyors. He ran along the length of the whale, measuring it with his tape, writing in his notebook.

Old Kra said he was the whaling inspector and that everyone in the fleet hated the sight of him. "He'd better watch out," Old Kra added, "or he'll end up with a broken head."

Old Kra quickly explained why during a brief pause when a cable broke. "A factory deck at full cook's a dangerous place for anyone, but especially dangerous for a whaling inspector. There's an inspector assigned to every ship by the whaling commission. They're supposed to enforce whaling laws. He's measuring to find out if the whales are of legal size. He has to log every whale in, give its species and size, and note whether it's a male or a female, when it was taken, and by what gunner. So he doesn't have a friend in the fleet."

"Why, what can he do if he finds illegal whale?" Erik asked.

"Nothing," said Old Kra. "Except send in a bad report to the whaling commission back home. Look at that poor little fellow. What can he do to enforce the law against nearly a thousand tough whalemen? Nothing. He can go back to Norway and report flagrant violations of the law. But I've never heard of any whaleman being arrested or fined for shooting a female whale with calf, or a short whale."

"Then why do they all hate the inspector so?" Erik asked.

"He's in the way, lad. Didn't I tell you the one big sin on this factory ship is holding up production? Well, that inspector's always in the way, measuring, arguing, slowing down production a little. So the whalemen wish he would get himself fed to the sharks. If he doesn't watch out, one of them will see that he does."

A little later the inspector hurried past the butcher decks toward the winch deck shouting something about a "short whale" and waving his tape measure angrily. As he passed the blubberboys, one of them shook his whale hook furiously at his back and shouted after him. "You useless snoop. If you want to inspect whale so much, take a good look at this!"

The blubberboy flicked his hook and sent a heavy slab of blubber spinning across the deck. It struck the inspector behind the knees, hurling him over backward onto the deck. He kept on going, spinning round and round, and only a looping guy wire stopped him from sliding down through a cooker hole into a vat of boiling fat.

Erik heard the man groan as he crawled away from the cooker hole. Then he collapsed into a pitiful, unconscious heap. The emergency siren blew, and two men appeared in the steam carrying a stretcher. They loaded the inspector onto it and hauled him below.

Old Kra shook his head grimly. "With a scarcity of whale, everybody's getting more and more desperate for oil. They will do anything to get more oil I guess: even murder an inspector if they can. Accidents are always happening on a butcher deck."

Another siren announced the resumption of production. Old Kra ran in with his hook, shouting. "You're learning all right, Orm, but you have to move faster. Faster, you understand?"

Erik nodded and ran in shakily, past the whirring blades of the slicers. He soon forgot all about inspectors and whaling laws and the possibility of accidents. He was too busy hooking and dragging at the endless stream of blubber that poured over from the flensers. By the time the blubberboys started to catch up, the siren signaled the arrival of more whale.

Erik pushed himself until his eyes blurred and his head rang, but when he stumbled or paused to catch his breath, Old Kra shouted: "Faster, faster!"

"I can't go any faster," panted Erik desperately.

"You'd better. We're falling behind the flensers. If that happens, we're in trouble."

Especially me, Erik thought, starting to panic. I'm on probation. Captain Haakonsson is up there just waiting for an excuse to ship me back to South Georgia.

In a kind of desperate lunge, he savagely pulled another chunk of blubber from the pile. Grease squirted from it as it slammed to the deck. This chunk kept going. Erik realized at once that he had pulled too hard, and that the ponderous mound of fat was plunging away from him—and in the wrong direction.

It was heading straight into the legs of the men who operated the slicing machines. If the blubber kept going in a straight line across the greasy deck, it would smash those men right into the whirring blades.

Erik tried to stop it. He held onto the hook, but the blubber pulled his weight easily after it over the grease-slick deck planks.

TEN

Erik gripped the hook with his left hand and flailed out with his right, trying to grab an anchoring hold somewhere. He shouted a warning, but his voice seemed lost in the roar of the machines.

He reached for a cable with his right hand and held to the hook with his left. But the weighty plunge of the blubber was too great. It tore the hook from his hand. He stared at the mound of fat slipping away from him, straight toward the slicing machines, his hook still quivering in it.

He jumped up and ran after it, knowing he could never overtake it in time. Old Kra hopped into view, his ragged coat flapping; he hooked the escaping blubber. Bracing his spiked boot soles into the deck planks, both arms out stiff, he swerved it neatly around to the left, using the momentum of its speed to direct it in a circle, back toward the cooker holes.

"Blubber up!" the old man shouted. Blubberboys in

the steam shouted back, "Blubber up!" Old Kra flicked his hook free of the slab, and another blubberboy caught the whirling lump on his hook and swung it to a third who swerved it to a fourth.

As the fat dropped from view, another blubberboy jerked out Erik's hook and tossed it to him with a warning yell. Erik made a wild jump and snagged it from a cloud of steam. But then he lost his footing when he hit the deck, and sprawled flat in a puddle of stinking *grax*, a foul mixture of blood, grease, and swill.

He jumped up at once, *grax* dribbling from his face and coat. Forcing himself forward again, he slapped his hook into another blubber slab. This time he eased it down carefully, and at the same time tried for more speed as he dug his heels into the deck like Old Kra and swung the blubber about at an angle for the nearest cooker hole.

"That's the way, lad," encouraged Old Kra. "But faster, faster now!"

Erik nodded and sighed and wondered how it was humanly possible to go faster. After what had happened, and what had almost happened, he was afraid to push himself. Risk doesn't matter though, he thought. Nothing matters here except speed, getting more whales cut up and into the cookers. He could never be good enough to please these veterans of the game, but he drove himself harder, while old men and scrawny kids raced embarrassing circles around him.

84

Erik's back throbbed with pain now when he tried to straighten up. His arms had stopped aching; they moved like wooden sticks, automatically but without feeling. He stumbled about in the hot steam and grease like a robot under someone else's control.

"Faster," pleaded Old Kra.

Sometime later Erik saw that the blubber pile was shrinking rapidly. Soon a last chunk of fat slithered into a cooker hole, and Old Kra said they could take a breather.

Erik slumped down on a rusted bollard, gasping for breath. His face stung from the scalding grease as if he'd been attacked by a hundred bees. His body ached everywhere like one big bruised fingernail.

No more whales were coming up the slipway. The whale that had just been flensed was being dragged on after the other carcasses toward the forward, or lemming, section of the butcher deck.

It made Erik feel a bit queasy. He looked away at the ocean and the glint of drifting icebergs until Old Kra's warning cry came again. Erik forced his protesting muscles back into action. Later, panting and gasping, he asked when they could take off long enough for a real rest, maybe a little sleep and a sandwich.

"When there are no more whale," Old Kra said.

Erik kept himself moving in a kind of daze, back and forth, over and over, round and round in the steam. He had no idea how many whales slid down to the lemming deck or how long he'd been dragging blubber. Nor did it matter, he thought. Oil was going into the tanks. Bonemeal and other products were piling up in the storage holds. The factory was going now at what they called "full-cook." This meant that a hundred-ton whale was being dragged aboard, processed and sent to the cookers every forty minutes. Each whale was worth six thousand dollars. And that was all, Erik knew, that meant anything to the whalemen.

Finally Old Kra's voice brought him out of his daze: "Rest while you can, lad. More whale pods coming in soon from Bornak."

Erik's legs quivered with fatigue as he shuffled carefully across the slippery deck to the port rail. He leaned there looking down at the clean cold wash of the sea and took deep breaths to ease that threat of nausea digging at his stomach.

He was beginning to feel better when he was jerked around by a sudden ripping shriek. He stared at the lemming deck, and slowly something in his stomach seemed to turn completely over.

Deblubbered carcasses of whale remained scattered over the forward lemming deck in various stages of dissection. They had piled up there after the blubber was stripped away, for that could be done much faster than the remaining tons of meat and bone could be cut up into small enough chunks to be squeezed through the cooker holes. While the flensing deck was resting, the lemmers still worked.

Whining cables swung the bone and flesh across the deck. Steam-driven bone saws bit into huge sides of whalemeat as big as house walls and through rib bones thicker than a man's body.

A winch cable tore tons of baleen, or whalebone, from a mouth and swung it over the side as discard. A massive backbone on a chain swung past Erik's head. One ligament was as thick and tough as a warship's anchor cable, with spinal vertebrae the size of tractor wheels.

Erik looked down for a moment at the dark pools of blood that were spreading all over the deck.

He bent over, twisted, and leaned over the rail. Dully, with a kind of bitter helpless anger, he knew he was being sicker than he had ever been in his life.

He remembered very little about his next go at the blubber. He stumbled through hours of grease and steam and waves of nausea as though through a bad dream. The one thing he noticed and cared strongly about was the fact that no one seemed to notice or care about him.

He was glad of that. They were not aware of his wretched sickness and weakness. If they had noticed it, they had shown no concern one way or another. The only time Erik drew any unfavorable attention was when he stopped hauling blubber. Then a frantic voice always screamed at him: "Faster, faster, lad. You want the flensers to bury us in blubber?"

"No," Erik said, and kept going.

"Nothing to be ashamed of, lad," Old Kra assured him once during a brief lull when a whale got stuck in the slipway. "The toughest man in this fleet turned green sick when he first saw a butcher deck at full-cook. Don't think about what you see and smell, lad. You'll soon be like all the rest of us, not smelling or seeing anything but the sight of more oil and money. Let me tell you, lad—all the butchery and killing and blood in the world won't matter, if you just stick with it long enough."

So Erik stuck with it. Soon he'd be cruising the clean cold sea along the fringe of the Weddell pack ice with Bornak, he told himself. And as Old Kra had promised, his mind and his stomach hardened. His nerves grew calloused. The sight and smell of blood and *grax* meant less and less.

And after weeks of dragging blubber, he was too numbed and stupefied by cold and exhaustion to feel anything, or care about anything . . . .

Shift followed monotonous, backbreaking shift. Shifts blurred into endless weeks. Life fell into a timeless, mindless blur of grease and steam. When whales stopped coming in, he stumbled like a sleepwalker down into the blubberboys' hold and fell dead asleep.

Regular watches were out. Erik worked when whales came in. When whales stopped coming in, he ate whatever food was around and went to sleep. He slept until the siren twisted him awake and then he again hauled blubber.

The blubberboys' hold lay directly under the wet, cold, and ever-dripping overhead deck plates. A convenient location—when the siren signaled the arrival of more whale, men could jump right up through the manhole and directly out onto the flensing deck. No time must be wasted getting at the blubber. But living conditions could not have been more miserable.

The hatches were kept battened and the scuttles secured, so that nowhere did fresh air enter. The damp made everything always cold and mildewed. The blubberboys were usually too tired to clean up much and often fell asleep still in heavy clothing, soggy with salt water and grease and drying whale blood.

Erik waited more and more anxiously for word from Bornak.

ELEVEN

Erik realized during the following weeks that he wasn't the only one interested in Bornak. Everyone, the whole fleet, worried about him. He had promised to send in plenty of big blue whales to the cookers. So far he had sent in none at all.

The fleet was falling behind fast on their oil quota, and only the profitable blues could make up the deficiency.

Erik felt the growing desperation of the men. A dangerous tension filled the blubberboys' hold. The oil quota had been set very high. If they went over their quota, they could return home with a reasonable paycheck for the six months of grueling work. If they didn't reach that quota, they would all go home broke.

And every day they fell further behind on their quota. Adding to their bitterness was the cold. It began to freeze men's fingers and faces. It froze their feet. Some screamed with pain of frostbite and were taken away to sick bay.

Smaller-sized whales came in fairly regularly, but small whales weren't enough.

Accidents and fatalities increased throughout the fleet. Bad luck and bad weather hardly improved the tempers of the men. A catcher, rammed by an iceberg, sank with all hands. Ten men were seriously injured on the butcher deck by falling shackles, falling ice, snapping cables, and flying fragments of broken bone-saw blades. A whale came loose from its anchoring cable on the flensing deck and crushed three men flat against the larboard rail. Two men were lost overboard during a hurricane.

The snow-laden gales, the ice, the thunderous seas, were the worst some of the old-timers had ever seen in *Zuther Notion.* And intelligence reports kept leaking hints that other whaling expeditions were having better luck, especially the hated Japanese and Russian fleets.

One night another Antarctic gale roared in. It blackened the sky and filled the world with freezing rain. The thermometer dropped suddenly to twenty-eight degrees below zero. All activity on the butcher deck came to a halt. Blubberboys stumbled below moaning with fatigue and cold.

Erik lay wide awake staring into the shadows of the

hold and listening to the howl of the wind and the thud of the sea. The storm eased up somewhat, but no more whales were coming in, and Erik tried to get some sleep while he had the chance. The ship was still rolling heavily though, and the winds blew at sixty miles an hour.

Suddenly Erik was wide awake. Jagged ice grinding along the *Arcturus'* hull had scared him out of sleep, and he lay there uneasily. He knew that the *Arcturus* had dropped anchor in the lee of an iceberg to escape the gale's force. But all of its thirty-thousand tons were tugging at the anchor chains, and the wind shivered its frame at the joints as if it were a rowboat. Erik shuddered as he thought of the thousands of miles of icy desolation surrounding them.

He managed to doze off, but he was torn from sleep again, this time by a blast of freezing air. It cut down through the stale heat and smell of the hold like a clean knife through rancid butter.

Erik rolled over, looking up at the open hatch. Sleet, snow, and saltwind whirled through the hold. Blubberboys rolled out of their greasy beds and shouted in angry protest. Then all of a sudden they stopped.

Bornak. The giant figure, familiar from many pictures Erik had seen, dropped through the hatch and landed in the hold with the ponderous ease of a polar bear. Yellow sea boots, a blue parka and fur cap glinted with ice crystals. Erik looked and stood up, and then he held his breath and kept on looking as though trying to be sure it was Bornak.

Bornak saw him, and his voice rumbled out of the shadows: "We're ready to hunt the blue whale, son of Egil."

Erik nodded slowly.

"Throw away that hook, Egil's son. You've seen the last of this rat's nest."

"I'm to come with you now?"

"Yah—I've checked you out with Captain Haakonsson. Everything's fixed. This is our sea now, lad. We gunners call the tune."

Erik grabbed up his foul-weather gear and put it on.

"Now get topside and let's move out," Bornak said. "That wind's liable to get mean." He laughed as though the sixty-mile-an-hour wind wasn't mean but some kind of a joke.

Erik grinned uneasily, nodded to Old Kra, and climbed up the ladder onto the deck ahead of Bornak. A blast of icy wind almost tore him off of his feet and he clung to a guy wire.

Bornak was shouting behind him. Erik stumbled on across the ice-slick deck to the lee of the ship. There, in a murky haze of spray and spume, he saw a sight that chilled his heart.

Ice was forming on the decks, wires, and cables of the *Arcturus*. The sea surged above the bulwark, bringing with it the looming hulk of *Catcher One*. The boat soared high above the level of the *Arcturus'* deck, and lashed with chains alongside the catcher's port gunwale was a sixty- or seventy-foot finner.

The whale had been killed by Bornak just to use as a fender. It was the only kind of fender that, in a sea such as this, could keep a five-hundred-ton boat from smashing itself to pieces against anything it might put alongside of. And even this seventy tons or so of fender was fast being battered into a rubbery mass as it slammed again and again into the *Arcturus'* hull.

A winch clattered weakly against the wind's howl. A frightened Norski deckhand tried to direct a netload of cargo over onto the catcher's deck. "Use the slingchair, man!" he shouted. "You're not going to jump—"

Bornak shoved the Norski out of his way. He looked at Erik and pointed up at the sea foaming high above the *Arcturus'* bulwark. The catcher and its whale fender rose on the peak of the swell. Then the sea dropped, and the catcher fell below the *Arcturus'* deck.

"When she rises again," Bornak shouted, grinning, "jump!"

Erik got hold of a guy wire and swung himself up onto the icy top of the bulwark. His spiked soles scraped and slipped on the rusted surface. Then he was squinting down through the stinging spray into the far-down boiling trough of the sea. He saw the top of the catcher and its fender bucking and twisting.

He wiped his eyes. The catcher started up again, cascading tons of water from her decks.

Jump onto the whale, he thought. You'll have to jump onto the whale first, then over the top of it onto the catcher.

It swelled up before him, the torn and battered carcass. It trembled and jerked in its chains as though struggling even in death to be free.

Erik hesitated almost too long. Then he hurled himself out and away, across the narrow, black, deadly canyon that separated the *Arcturus* from the whale.

TWELVE

Erik thought of himself ski jumping. He threw all of his weight forward as he went through the air so that when he landed his weight would go on falling forward, and not back and down between the whale and the *Arcturus'* hull.

He hit on the sloping side of the whale. He fell forward, digging with his spikes into the rubbery flesh. Then he sprang upward, first on one foot, then the other, and cleared the whale in another leap that took him onto the catcher's deck space atop the engine-room coping.

He let his legs fold under him, and he rolled his shoulders to take the brunt of the fall. He grabbed a taut cable for anchorage and pulled himself back up to his feet just as the catcher dropped sickeningly under him like an elevator.

Its tons of steel hit bottom on the trough of the sea

with a tremendous jolt, burying its nose and most of its bulwarks. Shaking itself loose, the boat rose again, its whale fender grinding and thudding on the wall of the *Arcturus'* hull. Bornak leaped into view over the rise of the whale. Then he dropped beside Erik, landing on all fours with heavy, poised ease.

At once Erik felt the vibrating roar of the engines. The catcher plunged out and away from the *Arcturus* like a black porpoise.

Sheets of spray slammed into Erik as he struggled aft after Bornak along the engine-room coping. Waves washed into his knees and almost battered him into the sea. One moment the catcher's stern plunged so deep into the waves that Erik wondered if it would come up again. Then it was shaking its entire fifteen-foot depth free in an explosion of spray.

Bornak squeezed down a narrow companionway and stepped through a doorway. As Erik dropped after him, he was momentarily frozen by a sight he was to remember ever afterward with terror.

The dead whale's torn and battered carcass, released from its chains, was drifting away to starboard. Its torn flukes swayed feebly as it sank from sight, as though some faint bit of life still rippled in it. Behind one of the many giant icebergs, drifting everywhere now before the screaming wind, lay the *Arcturus* rolling dangerously beneath ice cliffs in a haze of mingled sea, scud, and black clouds. The air was filled with the constant crunch and thunder of ice pans grinding nearer and nearer.

Erik followed Bornak down the companionway, through the doorway, and along a passage to a tiny compartment. A yellow bulb brightened and dimmed with each roll of the catcher, shining on rusted bulkheads, a steel bunk, footlocker, small table, and a bench.

"This was a storage room," Bornak said, "but I cleaned it out for you. The son of Egil deserves good gunner's accommodations. More important, you need a private and quiet place to work in."

Erik couldn't imagine what sort of work an apprentice gunner would do in this windowless cell. Maybe Bornak thought he still needed to study books on whaling. He would soon find out that Erik already knew all he could learn from books. What he needed now was a chance at the harpoon gun.

Bornak walked to the steel footlocker and started unlocking the padlock. Erik envied the giant's easy balance. The catcher's roll and pitch forced Erik to hold hard to the frame of his bunk. The catcher had none of the solid feel of the big factory ship's decks. It rode like a cork, and Erik knew he'd need a while to get his proper sea legs.

He pulled a blanket around his shoulders, but the freezing wind, that terrifying leap, and the more terrifying look at the storming sea seemed to have caught up with him. He felt as if he had bubbles in his blood and ice in his bones, and his teeth kept clicking together.

Melted ice dripped from Bornak's beard as he pulled something out of the footlocker. He held a black leather-bound book in his hand. It looked like a log-book.

"You'll have to do some paperwork before we can go on the big hunt, Egil's son."

"Why?" Erik said. "My father taught me everything about shooting whales that a gunner needs to know."

"I'm sure he did, but now you have to study about how to *find* whales, not about how to shoot them." Bornak spoke in a low, tense voice. He gripped the black-bound notebook so hard with both hands that the tendons and veins bulged in his wrists like cables.

"Don't worry about becoming a gunner, Egil's son. I promised you that, and you'll chase all the big fish you can shoot. I'll give you your ten contract shots and your gunner's certificate. Don't worry. The fact that Bornak trained you is enough to make you a famous harpooner." He tapped the logbook with thick fingers. "No, this is something else. This fleet depends on me to make its oil quota. I have to find plenty of big blues as I said I would, yah. But I must depend on you, Egil's son. Without you, I cannot find the blue whales."

Erik blinked slowly three times. "Why would you have to depend on me to find blue whales?"

"The information's here," Bornak said, and he handed the logbook to Erik. "It's here, and only you can figure it out."

Erik stared and felt his eyes blur and sting a little as he looked at the faded gold letters on the cover:

CATCHER TWO

Gunner Captain Egil Nordahl

"My—father's logbook," Erik whispered after a long stillness.

"Yah. When I found him after his last fight with the blue whale, his catcher was sunk, his crew gone. He had salvaged only this logbook. As he was dying, he asked me to do two things. First, I was to train you as a gunner. Second, I was to keep this logbook a secret from all others, keep it with me until I could give it to you. He wanted you and me to be partners and go after the big blues in the greatest whale hunt the world will ever see!"

Erik shook his head slowly. He waited.

"Your father found what all whalemen have dreamt of finding since Norwegian hunters first invaded the southern ice fields. He found the secret hidden sea and breeding grounds of the great blue whale."

Erik looked at the cover of the logbook, then up at Bornak's tense waiting face, then down again at the logbook. His hands were not quite steady. Bornak's voice wasn't steady either, and his eyes seemed abnormally bright: "You've heard of the hidden sea of the blue whale?"

Erik nodded. "Yes, but I thought it was just a myth, one of those tall stories whalemen like to tell. More like a legend, like the graveyard of the elephants they used to say was somewhere in Africa."

"I don't know about any graveyard of the elephants in Africa, but I do know there is a hidden sea of blue whale in Antarctica. Thousands, maybe millions of whale are there—giant blues, all the great blues left in the world. We're the only ones who'll know where they are, Egil's son. Only we will be able to go there. Only we can hunt that sea. We will be able to kill blues as fast as we can shoot. We'll kill more and bigger blues than any hunter that has ever lived or ever will live."

"Why does it depend on me?" Erik asked thickly.

"The directions for finding the sea are there, written in the Nordahl gunner code. You're the only person in the world now that your father is dead who knows that code. You're the only one who can decipher it now."

Erik looked at the logbook, and felt working inside him a strange aching mixture of exultation and fear.

"You can translate that code all right?" Bornak's voice was loud with tension.

Erik nodded. "I learned the Nordahl code, of course. I've translated a few short practice messages, but that's all. A more complicated message might take some time —I mean it might be sort of hard to work out."

"But you can do it! You can do it you said!"

"Yes, I just said it might not be too easy. When do we have to have the directions worked out?"

"The sooner the better, yah? We've already had to put off the big hunt too long."

"Why have we put it off then?" Erik said. "Why did you leave me on the butcher deck so long?"

"I wanted to get on the whalemen's nerves," Bornak said, grinning. "I wanted them to worry and fret, to work themselves into a near mutiny worrying about not getting whale, not finding any blues. I wanted them to get so worked up they'd do anything to get whales. Getting whales depends on me. When I walked into Captain Haakonsson and told him who you were and that I wanted you aboard my catcher as an apprentice gunner, what could he do but say yes? He had to say yes. Everyone in this fleet will now have to say yes to Bornak if they want whale. When I give the word, they'll follow me anywhere if I promise them whale—they'll follow me into the worst seas in *Zuther Notion*."

Erik opened the logbook. As he turned the pages, his hands trembled. Seawater had stuck many of the pages together, had blurred the ink on others, so that much of the writing was illegible. "I might not be able to find the coded message in here," he said.

"I found the code already," Bornak growled impatiently. "All of it seems to be at the back—on the last few pages of the book. Don't bother with the rest of the pages. They mean nothing. They're filled with the same ordinary day-to-day log entries made by all captains— weather, position, number of whales sighted and taken. No, we're only interested in those last few pages, Erik. Those are the entries your father made just after he found the hidden sea, and just before he was killed."

Erik started to turn to the back of the logbook, but he stopped and stared at the rusting bulkhead of the compartment. He listened to the howl of the wind and the driving sea, and a chill went down his back as though he'd been touched with ice.

"Something troubling you, Erik?"

"You were with my father when he died?"

"Yah. I told you that. He entrusted the logbook to me. I was to keep it safe until you and I together could use it and go on the big hunt. His last words to me were that I should train you as a gunner and—"

"Yes," Erik interrupted, "but how did he die?"

"What do you mean?" Bornak said quickly.

"What really happened? The letter sent home by Captain Haakonsson only said that he was killed when his catcher was wrecked by a blue whale."

"Yah, what really happened," Bornak mumbled. He flexed his huge hands and looked impatiently at the logbook. "We got an SOS from Egil on the edge of the Weddell Sea. The message said that Egil's catcher had been dragged into the ice by a blue whale. Its hull was peeled open, and it was sinking. We had a rough time getting there through the ice floes. When we did get there, the catcher had gone down with all hands except your father. He'd managed to escape onto an ice floe, but he was dying. He lived only a few minutes after we reached him."

"He told you he'd found the hidden sea of the blue whale," Erik said slowly, "that its location was in Nordahl code and that we should break the code and hunt that sea together?"

"Yah, yah," Bornak said, his voice rising with impatience. "It's there at the back of the book. You read it. He mentions the hidden sea and the Enderby Quadrant and the code. It's all there, Erik."

Erik opened the logbook at the back and quickly scanned a few paragraphs of his father's writing. "The code's scattered and hidden through several pages of notes. Digging it out and putting it together won't be easy."

"But you can do it, yah, yah?"

Erik nodded solemnly. "It'll take some time, that's all."

"We have some time, Erik. Once we find the hidden sea, we can shoot more whale in a few weeks than we could otherwise shoot all season." Bornak laughed loudly. "Right now you need a little rest, some sleep."

"I could use some sleep all right, sir."

"You do that, Egil's son. Go to the galley, and Ollie'll fry you up a thick whalesteak."

Erik looked up from the logbook and nodded. "I'll work it out as fast as I can, sir."

"Good. Now—" Bornak got a map from the footlocker, spread it out on the table, and pointed to a section north of the Antarctic continent and south of Bouvet Island. "Here is a section of sea just off Enderby Land. Egil was in this area somewhere when he crashed into the ice. He was always cruising this area, and there were rumors that he was looking for the hidden sea of blues here. Well, he was here when he crashed and was making those final entries in his log, so we can be pretty sure that the hidden sea is in the Enderby Quadrant somewhere. That's a big wilderness of unexplored sea. It also happens to be one of the most dangerous and most treacherous seas in the world."

Bornak stared down at the map, and his face was grim. "But it'll make us both famous and rich, Erik. Knowing the hidden sea's in this quadrant somewhere, I can set our course in that direction, even before you translate the code for the exact location of our goal."

"Yes, I see," Erik said.

"We'll sail there while you work out the code. That way we'll save time. When we see whale on the way, we'll shoot them. You will watch, Erik. You will be on the gunner's deck with me, and you will learn to kill whale as only Bornak, king of gunners, knows how to kill whale."

Erik was too stunned and excited to say anything more.

Bornak laughed and slapped him on the back. "You're eager to kill the big fish. Right, Egil's son?"

Erik managed a kind of mumbled agreement.

"I know that great feeling, Erik, waiting to sight your first whale. Whoever forgets the end of his first big fish, eh?" Bornak backed to the compartment door and opened it. "But the most important thing right now is that code. The fleet depends on those blue whales now for its oil quota."

"Yes, sir. I'll get right on it."

"Keep your work on the code a secret, Erik. Trust no one, not even Tiburon. Other whaling companies with fleets here would pay a fortune to any man who could furnish them the location of that hidden sea. Tell no one then. Trust no one."

"Yes, sir."

Bornak looked at the logbook once again, then went out slamming the steel door behind him.

One big mystery was now cleared away, Erik thought. The mystery of why Bornak had been so insistent on Erik not revealing his identity as Erik Nordahl, and why Bornak had not wanted to be seen with Erik or connected with him in any way until now when it was safe.

Other whaling companies, other gunners, would pay a fortune or commit murder, Erik knew, to learn the location of the hidden sea of the blues. Bornak had been afraid that others might suspect that Egil Nordahl had found that hidden sea, and that his son, Erik, knew the secret of its location.

Bornak didn't want anyone to get hold of me, Erik thought, and get the secret code out of me before he did.

Tell no one. Trust no one else. What about Tiburon? Did Tiburon know? Did anyone else know about the hidden sea and the code, Erik thought, but Bornak and I?

Erik was soon to find out that no one else did know. Bornak trusted no one.

THIRTEEN

Erik ate; he slept. He worked on the code. He puzzled over the symbols hour after hour with feverish impatience.

His eyes began to ache and burn with fatigue under the feeble light. His head throbbed. But he forced himself to struggle on.

Radio-telephone communications between the whale catchers and their mother factory ship are usually conducted in secret code. This code is shared by all fleet members. It stops information about the location of whale hunting grounds and other vital data from being intercepted by competing fleets.

Private codes, too, are used within a fleet. These belong to the old gunner families of Norway, and they are known by no one else. The skills of hunting and harpooning whales are jealously guarded secrets, handed down only from father to son. Such a code is especially valuable when several gunner captains of the same family all work for the same fleet. Then when one of them spots a choice hunting ground, he sends out his position by radio-telephone in the private code of his particular gunner clan. Thus only the members of his own family will share the kills, and the profits, with him.

The Nordahl code was one of the oldest and most difficult to decipher. Erik had never been in the Antarctic with his father, so he had not had any real opportunity to use the code. But he finally managed to translate several paragraphs into intelligible script. Regular diary entries were mixed with code, so that whole pages had to be decoded to make any sense.

Erik read what he had deciphered with growing wonder:

" . . . the blue whale's hidden sea and breeding ground has been a myth, so-called, a legend among whalemen for centuries. Whalemen have dreamt of finding it, but it has never been proven to exist.

"Still, I've always felt this sea to be a fact. The giant blues migrate every year. In winter they go north by the untold thousands, and in summer they return to the Antarctic to feed and breed. Maybe the old ones go there to die.

"Blue whale are highly intelligent, probably the smartest mammals on earth, next to man. They are smarter than apes and baboons, smart enough to have changed migration routes and formed special convoy systems in an attempt to avoid being slaughtered by hunters.

"They have also been smart enough, it seems, to have disappeared—what is left of them—from the Antarctic seas. Blues are the biggest, the most profitable to kill, so most of them have been slaughtered. But thousands remain. Where have they disappeared to? I believe that to avoid being exterminated they have hidden out in the legendary secret sea. They've always gone there to feed and breed. Now they hide there and do not come out until they have to.

"Another clue: Their food consists of billions and billions of red krill. Imagine the number of these tiny shrimp that a 120-ton blue whale needs just to stay alive! Alive, and also stored up with enough energy-fat to last many months while it swims north to the other end of the world! I've found traces of a warm water current in the Enderby Quadrant. Perhaps such a great warm stream cuts through the ice somewhere and leads to the hidden sea of the blues, somewhere behind the ice barrier. Krill must have such warm water if they are to thrive and multiply—in numbers so vast they can feed thousands, and have fed millions, of giant blue whales.

"I've searched and I'm still searching for that hidden sea. I work on the theory that it must be along the route traveled by the krill in this warm-water current. Each hunting season here in the Antarctic there are less and less blues. Last season only a few were sighted. Where else have the survivors gone but to their secret sea?

"I am taking my catcher again into the Enderby Quadrant. I'm going to follow up that trace of warm current. I intend to follow it wherever it takes me beyond the Weddell Sea. . . ."

His excitement about what his father had found drove Erik on until his eyes burned and he began to see double and the ache behind his eyes throbbed like a bruise.

He transposed letters and numbers. He transposed them again. In an hour he had managed to translate only a few lines of the code. Trembling with exhaustion and frustration, he pounded the tabletop and rubbed angrily at his eyes. The writing faded in and out of focus. He forced his head up and his eyes open.

He had only a dim memory of slumping across the table and hearing the distant sound of the logbook striking the deck. . . .

Then a kind of rusty scream pulled him out of his exhausted sleep. It was the wail of the siren followed by a voice blaring from the Tannoy speaker: *"Hvalblast! Hvalblast!"*

There she blows. The call to action. The sighting of the world's biggest game. Erik's hands gripped the table edge, and he stared at the Tannoy overhead.

"Out all hands! Out all hands . . . and apprentice gunner Nordahl please report at once to the gunner's deck!"

Erik gave an inarticulate cry and forced himself out of the chair. He grabbed up whatever clothing was at hand—khaki shirt, sweater, corduroy pants, fleece-lined leather flying jacket, woolen socks, thigh boots turned down below the knees, gloves, and a fur cap with earmuffs. He dressed and ran topside to the deck and forward to the midships superstructure.

The storm was gone. The weather was calm now, though very cold. Light clouds puffed along smartly on a southeast breeze. The bluish-green sea was broken only by small ripples. But as Erik ran, the plunging catcher was seized with a kind of feverish urgency.

The entire crew popped into view from every opening, fore and aft. Peering with binoculars and with the naked eye, they ran about in all directions trying to sight the whale.

"*Hvalblast!*" the lookout kept shouting from the barrel high atop the weaving masthead. He waved his fur cap and pointed three points off the starboard bow. "*Hvalblast . . .*"

Erik looked to starboard. *Catcher One* was cruising eastward along the fringe of the pack ice that surrounded the entire continent. A waste of sea stretched away in every direction, broken only by small bits of pack ice strung out in the wake of the storm, and icebergs drifting and glittering in the brittle sunlight.

Erik climbed up onto the bridge. It wasn't a warm enclosed area like the bridge of an ordinary ship. It was raw and open. Catcher men would stand there through the worst Antarctic weather, protected only by thick clothing. They needed a clear view. Moisture and sun distortion on glass-enclosed walls might cause them to miss a distant whale's spout.

An old sea dog of a Shelty stood at the wheel, solid and unmoving as sculpture. "Welcome aboard, Egil's son," he said. "I am Schulstock."

Erik nodded and faced the gunner's deck. His eyes teared in the cold wind as he looked down the narrow-railed catwalk. It led from the top of the bridge, over the entire foredeck to the high bow. The bow was knife-sharp, widely flared, and filled by a triangular steel platform. High in the forward point of this triangle stood the harpoon gun.

The lookout was shouting again. He pointed more to larboard now. The catcher abruptly changed course heading in the direction of the sighted whale. Its engines vibrated, and the blunt prow soon cut through the sea at double the ordinary plodding eight knots.

Erik leaned into the wind, his head spinning to the engine's roar. A voice boomed behind, "Where? Where now?" Turning, he saw Bornak jutting up against the sky above the bridge.

"There!" The lookout pointed. *"Hvalblast."*

Bornak called down the bridge phone to the engine-room, "Full speed ahead." He waved direction signals to Schulstock at the helm. "Steady as she goes."

Schulstock nodded.

"McDun!" Bornak shouted down to the foredeck. The engineer jumped down behind the main-deck winch. Its big wheels clanked, and the massive drum began to revolve, grinding up whale line from the hold —thousands of feet of rope, six inches thick.

Crewmen opened hatches, cranked levers, cleared lines, and broke out flagging and buoy markings.

Bornak vaulted the bridge railing to the catwalk. Turning, he pounded Erik on the back with a big fur-gloved hand. "Eager, eh. First-kill fever." His small eyes were keen and bright with excitement. "We'll get our big fish all right, Bornak doesn't miss. And he has the best crew in *Zuther Notion:* McDun, Schulstock, Thorder, Sigrid, Borgen." He hesitated, then turned away toward the gun as he mumbled, "Tiburon."

Erik looked down from the bridge to the foredeck. Tiburon stood near the winch drum. He touched his hand to his forehead and looked up at Erik. "All right, prince of gunners. You asked for it. Now let's see how you like it."

Erik shrugged; he turned away and vaulted the railing onto the catwalk after Bornak.

"They'll all be watching the son of Egil," Bornak called back to him. "They expect big things of you."

On the gun platform Erik helped Bornak uncover and unlock the harpoon gun. Bornak swung the barrel up and around to test it. Though heavy, its fine balance made it as maneuverable as a toy.

Bornak kicked open a steel box bolted to the deck. Inside glittered iron bombs packed in sawdust. "Do you know how to load?"

"Of course," Erik said.

He heaved up a soft-iron bomb with both hands and screwed it into the harpoon head. The head was already loaded into the cannonlike barrel. His father had made him load and unload until he could do it almost unconsciously. He tightened and locked in the bomb and checked the powder charge in the cannon's breech.

"Good," Bornak approved. He called up to the lookout. "Which way? Where now?"

"Right ahead still."

Erik squinted into the blinding spray, searching for his first sight of a whale. The horizon rose and fell. The catcher's every plunge hurled foam across the sky.

Erik saw it then. As the catcher lifted to top another swell, mist spouts rose between two distant waves.

Erik gripped the railing near the gun with both hands. His mouth worked several times, but no sound came out as he watched those two vertical spouts. Like feathery mist, wind-curved at their crests, they were the moisture of the whale's exhaled breath condensing in the air.

It came out of Erik in a faint whisper, *"Hvalblast . . ."*

Bornak laughed. "Louder, Egil's son. Shout loud and clear. Let the whale know it's met its master!"

Erik pointed at a mark off the starboard bow. This time his shout seemed to tear the lining from his throat. *"Hvalblast!"*

"Yah, yah!" Bornak said, staring to starboard. "I see it. What does it say?"

Erik took a quick nervous breath. As an apprentice, he knew, he was on the spot. They would be measuring how much he knew and how fast he would learn—

He studied the shape of the two spouts carefully. Two of them all right, he thought. He tried to dredge up from his mind everything that he had ever learned about spotting and identifying whale. That, he knew, was one of the most important things in a chase: the quick identification of the type of quarry you're up against. Every whale's habits are different. Every species runs and fights in its peculiar way. Each has its own speed, its own sounding and broaching habits. A successful chase depends on knowing immediately what you're after. An error in judgment can mean the loss of a whale, Erik reminded himself. And one whale is worth a hundred barrels of oil. One whale is worth six thousand dollars.

Pictures and diagrams that his father had made him study appeared in his mind:

The sperm whale's spout juts forward from its nose at a forty-five degree angle.

The right whale. It has a double spout.

The humpback. Its spout is short and fat.

The finback. Its spout is like that of the blue. It is vertical and narrowly funneled in still air.

But the blue whale's spout is shorter and broader than the finner's. The blue's spout isn't so narrow at the bottom, and it doesn't spread up and out gradually to a height of fifty feet above sea level.

Tall ghostly growths, these were, spreading out at their tops by the wind until they looked like frosted palm trees.

"Finners," Erik said.

"You sure?"

Erik gulped. "Er—yes, sir. Pair of them, sir. Finbacks—"

"We will soon see if you are right."

Erik noticed Tiburon watching him intently from the bridge. Erik turned away. Something about Tiburon's scrutiny made him uneasy and uncertain.

FOURTEEN

Erik braced himself against the gun platform railing
and watched Bornak. The king gunner moved with
cool and practiced skill. He tested the gun's grip and
sighted down the barrel. He checked the nylon leader
line. Five hundred feet and two hundred pounds of it lay
coiled on the gun platform at Erik's feet. It ran from
the harpoon head to the thousands of feet of massive,
six-inch Manila hemp rope that made up the main line.

"*En sildror!*" the lookout shouted.

The entire crew heard it and cheered loudly. Erik let
out a long sigh of relief. The lookout had verified that
the whales were finbacks. Erik had passed his first big
test. The whalemen were happy. Finners were next in
size to the fat blues. These were finners all right, swimming peacefully and unhurriedly about a quarter of a
mile ahead of the catcher.

They exhaled, or blew, their misty spouts at fairly

regular intervals of ninety seconds. But as the catcher drew within a hundred yards of them, they refused to dive, to sound.

"Sound, you stupid fish!" Bornak shouted, shaking his fist. "Don't waste my time."

Erik suddenly felt the immense strength and beauty of the finbacks. He had read about chasing and shooting whales, but he had never imagined what the animals would look like rolling through the sea.

How graceful they were, moving with such power and ease. Their horizontal flukes churned as the enormous tails plunged up and down, and at the same time from side to side in titanic rotary convolutions. Finners could furrow the sea at twenty knots. They often outran fast catchers and escaped into the ice floes.

This pair, however, continued to move along at a leisurely pace. They seemed uninterested in escape or flight. They showed no signs of fear. Apparently, Erik thought, they expect no harm from us.

They breakfasted casually on shoals of fish and krill. They swam on the surface of the sea, their enormous shoveling jaws open wide and taking in thousands of fish and tiny shrimp.

Between meals they played games. It took Erik awhile to realize that the huge whales were actually playing, having fun like any other creature that enjoys being alive. He watched at first with disbelief, then with an uneasy sort of resentment. Nearly two hundred tons of animal were leaping and frolicking about like dolphins, or like big happy dogs playing on a lawn. They dived in cascades of foam. They rolled over and over and nipped at one another. They leaped high into the air over one another in a kind of Herculean leapfrog.

Bornak shook both fists at them now and shouted with rising anger above the wind, "Stop playing games." He glared back at Erik. "See, they're having so much fun playing they don't care about us. They have to sound," Bornak shouted at Erik. "Why is that?"

"You can get in closer for a better shot after they dive," Erik said. "If they stay on the surface, they keep just a little too far ahead of you for a sure shot. But if they sound, then you can figure just where they'll surface again. You can be there, right where they come up."

"Yah, yah! If they're scared, they dive. Then they have to have air. They breathe air into their lungs just like we do, so they have to come up to the surface every few minutes. When they do that, we're there, you see. Then we can't miss. It's like hitting the side of a wall. You can't miss then unless your gun jams."

He turned away from Erik, back toward the gun. "Sound, sound you stupid fish!"

But the finners refused to sound. They played and sported, moving just fast enough to stay ahead of the catcher, never coming near enough for a sure shot.

Bornak called down the phone to the engine room. "Turn on the whale scarer." This was a new device Erik had only heard about. It gave out ultrasonic vibrations that prodded whales with fear, forcing them to sound and run until they were out of breath and had to come up faster and more often for air. This was supposed to make it easier to get in close for as many sure shots as you needed.

"One of these finners is a big one," Bornak said, peering ahead into the spray. "Eighty feet if he's an inch. I'd guess the little one is the son of the big one. Families usually travel and stay together. The mother's probably been killed. This is a very good way to make easy kills, Erik. Whale families stick together and try to help one another when they're in trouble. If you kill one, the others hang around to help or try to help."

Another half an hour passed before the finners finally sounded. Then suddenly they stopped their tremendous leaping and playing in the waves. Their splendidly broad and tapering backs arched high into the air, and they plunged straight down into the deep.

They surfaced very soon, though, blowing hard and filling the sky with mist. Evidently the whale scarer had jolted them only slightly. Now they were no more than a hundred feet from the catcher, though still not close enough for Bornak. He was crouching near the gun, swaying his shoulders and crooning. "Sound, sound now, you overgrown lummoxes. Once more now, dive!"

They did, suddenly and in unison. Their sleek tons

shot up. Their great tails reared high, and the whales speared straight down, the sea swirling and sucking over the snap of their flukes as if a ship had floundered and gone under there.

"How far, how fast, Egil's son?" Bornak said, "Which way? What speed?"

On the spot again, Erik gripped the railing hard with one hand. He took a slow careful breath. This was the most crucial test of a gunner's skill.

His father's words leaped into his mind. He tried to remember everything he had ever read about this part of the hunt:

"Real skill with the harpoon isn't so much being able to shoot straight. It's knowing where the whale will surface and when.

"The greatest of whales has no chance against steel whale catchers. The whale soon gets frantic for air, just as you or I would. The whale must surface or drown. You learn to be right there, and you scare it into diving as often as you want. You keep forcing the whale under until it is out of breath. Its lungs bursting for air, it comes up often, and so close to you that you may hit it as easily and as many times as you please. . . ."

What else, what else? Erik thought. How far? How fast?

". . . the length of time whales stay down after sounding varies according to species, and to the degree of their fear. Know in what direction the whale goes while beneath the surface; also know its speed; then you can judge where and when it will surface.

"Figure well; the whale should breach less than fifteen yards from your catcher. Then you have about half a minute in which to fire before the whale dives again.

"But if it does dive again, don't worry. You have scared the animal and it is short of breath. It will have to come up again soon and quite near. This time you will have less trouble getting closer for an even better shot.

"The scared blue whale breaches twelve times at twelve- to fifteen-minute intervals. A finner's regular full broach time is fifteen minutes. It makes a full broach only when it is very, very scared, and before it is very winded. A single tickle from a whale scarer won't frighten a whale very much, at least not the first time. . . ."

This pair of finners, Erik reasoned, is only slightly scared. They will breach soon. They will probably travel underwater at about a third of their maximum speed of twenty knots. They should surface in about a third of their full diving time of fifteen minutes. They aren't frightened enough to stay under much longer. They will be traveling at about six knots.

And they will, Erik concluded his calculations, keep swimming in the general direction in which they were moving when they sounded. That white shadow extending in an almost straight line through the water is an undersea stream of krill. The whales will follow the krill, so they can feed while they swim.

Quickly he told Bornak his conclusion. Bornak nodded and asked, "When will they breach then?"

"Five minutes," Erik stammered. "No, make it six. No, make it about seven or—"

"Trust your hunches," Bornak interrupted. "If you know, your first guesses are usually right. If you don't know, you're wasting time."

"Five, it is," Erik said.

Bornak called down to the engine room for more speed. He called up to Schulstock to steer ahead south-southeasterly along the edge of the pack ice.

The catcher swerved to port into lengthening swells. Its engines labored harder. A few minutes later Bornak called for half speed. They slid along more easily then. Penguins and seals squawked and barked at them from nearby icebergs as they passed.

Erik waited with growing tension. The crew were watching him, waiting to judge his worth. He knew they were, whether they seemed to be noticing him or not.

FIFTEEN

A little more than five minutes later the whales surfaced.

Erik felt that the crew's happy shouts were partially for him, and he straightened proudly, grinning and feeling like a prizefighter who had just won round two.

Bornak slammed his hands flat on the gun barrel again, a habit of his. Erik fell back against the railing, awed by the looming nearness of the finners. They emerged from the waves like two newly forming reefs. Tons of water cascaded from their sides, and sheets of icy spray drenched the ship.

Erik wiped at his face and half-blinded eyes. Waves from the rearing finners buffeted the big steel catcher as if it were a floating bottle.

Its wild pitching meant little to Bornak. He seemed to notice very little but the harpoon gun. Balanced easily, he seized the pistol grip in his right hand. Signaling to Schulstock with his left hand, he shouted into the phone. "Astern! Astern . . . half speed!"

He crouched and peered down the barrel, waiting to fire. "Wait now, wait my fat fish," he crooned. "Hold it now . . . easy . . . easy does it now . . . higher up into the air . . . that's right . . . a bit higher now, my fat old finner. . . ."

They rose up and up effortlessly, until the head of the giant finner towered fifty feet above the bow and was only about fifteen feet away. Bornak waited. Erik felt a terrible tightening as though a rope were being pulled taut around his belly. The finners rose higher, and higher still.

"Boooommm!"

The crash of an explosion roared in Erik's head. He looked up, stunned, to see the yellow nylon leader darting away across the gun platform after the flying harpoon. Black smoke from the explosion was swirled over the deck.

Bornak released the gun while the harpoon was still arching through the air toward the whale. He locked it and flung himself at the phone.

"Easy as she goes! Astern full speed. Keep her tight and astern full!" His voice rose to a hoarse bellow: *"We've got fast fish . . . fast fish!"*

126

The crew let out an answering roar of triumph: "Fast fish ... fast fish ..."

"You figured right, son of Egil. You found us plenty of fish," shouted Thorder.

"Hit it again, Bornak!" urged Schulstock from the bridge.

The large finner had a 160-pound harpoon iron buried three feet in its flesh. It lunged about trying to free itself from the barbed shaft. It churned up the sea, but its efforts only increased its pain.

Bornak called down to the engine room, and to the helmsman and the men at the windlass.

"Booommmmmm!"

The second explosion seemed to come from nowhere and everywhere at once, and then from all over the sea. There was something muffled about it, and horrible. Then Erik knew what it was. It was the sound of the time-fused iron bomb going off deep inside the whale's body.

The finner arched up in a spasm of agony as its vital organs tore. Its twelve-foot tail flew high above the catcher. Its length went straight up, then down. It disappeared into the depths, and the smaller whale dove after it.

"Half speed astern, half speed astern!" Bornak ordered. The nylon leader sped away in graceful uncoiling curves. Its five-hundred-foot length soon played out. The six-inch main line began pouring out after it then, unwinding from the spinning winch drum on the foredeck.

McDun played the whale as an ordinary landlubber might play a trout. But instead of a small rod and reel, McDun used a thick rope and a huge steam-driven winch attached to a five-hundred-ton catcher.

Thousands of additional feet of rope lay coiled in the hold below deck. The line began to roar and whip away from the winch drum. Faster, faster it went out. It smoked and screamed as the whale dived straight down.

Five-, six-, seven-hundred feet of line went down. The whale continued its dive.

The rope ran through its well-sprung blocks, then around the winch drum and through the tray before the gun, and so to the harpoon and the whale.

"A thousand feet down now," Bornak shouted. The whale kept diving deeper.

Erik watched the line lashing into the sea's depths. The whale swam down there in a senseless fury of pain, wanting only to escape. But it is useless, Erik thought. The whale has to come up for air. No matter how deep it goes, it can never escape the barb and the fatal injury of bombs exploding in its body.

And we'll be waiting, Erik thought.

And it was then that he felt the first dim stirrings of protest. The feeling was faint but unmistakable. It was like a dull ache spreading through his belly, then a kind of revulsion or sickness, as if he'd eaten stale food.

He was ashamed of the feeling and determined to

128

ignore it. It is the same sickness I felt on the butcher's deck, he thought. Yes, that was all that ailed him, and he would soon get over it, just as he had gotten over the nausea he'd felt when he saw his first whale butchered. He kept telling himself this until the feeling began to ease away.

The next half hour seemed like five hours to Erik. Finally the pulley began to slow. The winch stopped more often. With over half a mile of line out, the finner's great vitality finally wore down. McDun could reel the whale in.

Bornak looked at Erik. "Don't just stand there! Move! Move and reload, you hear? You should have had another bomb in by this time. Load, load!"

Erik nodded. That dangerous warning fluttered again in his stomach. Slowly and carefully he got hold of the bomb and fitted it into the harpoon head.

He stumbled back to the security of the railing. Out of the corner of his eye, he saw several members of the crew watching him. Schulstock and the two called Thorder and Sigrid were looking at him with a kind of impersonal interest. Yes, he thought, that's what it was —impersonal. They didn't know him. They didn't care about him personally. They were just interested in whether he would come through or not, whether he could make the grade.

Tiburon was studying him, too, but at least Tiburon

looked at him as if he were a person, a living human being, and not just an object in someone's experiment.

Erik drew himself up. He was supposed to be a prince of gunners, the son of a king of gunners. He was a Nordahl, and the Nordahls had been famous gunners for generations.

But he didn't feel like one. How could a gunner feel dizzy and weak because of a whale's dying?

He remembered what Tiburon had told him on the Tönsberg docks:

"Sure, but you've never seen a hundred tons of whale blowing blood. You never saw a big part of God's sea turned red as sin. Until you see a bomb shot into a heart weighing half a ton, you don't know anything about whaling."

Erik shook himself out of the daze. Bornak was rechecking the harpoon and bomb. He ignored Erik. He acted as though everything was going along normally.

"Ready, all ready," he said, leaning on the gun breech.

Erik took several slow deep breaths of cold air. Maybe this weakness of mine is in my imagination, he told himself. I had a weak stomach for the butcher decks, but I got over that. If I stick with this, I'll become hardened to killing whales, too. The more he thought of it the better he felt, and then the high excitement of the hunt surged up in him again and pushed aside his doubts.

The dripping line had sagged. The winch reeled in hundreds of yards of rope with little resistance from the whale. "Haul away," Bornak ordered. "You're in for it now, daddy fish."

Erik watched as the dripping rope came out of the sea. The wounded whale lunged up about a hundred yards distant. It was exhaling desperately, sucking at precious air. Its spout was like a broken fountain over the waves.

"Slower," growled Bornak into the phone. "Keep that line straight."

The whale was still swimming along the surface, blowing irregularly, weakly. The catcher picked up speed to counter the anticipated pull if the finner took up the slack again in another frenzied effort.

And the rope did, incredibly, snap taut once more. The shock ran through the steel of the ship, seemed to wrench its rivets loose.

Then it was happening—an incredible and over-whelming feat of strength and vitality and will to fight: The wounded dying animal was pulling the five-hundred-ton catcher with the catcher's engines pulling in full reverse!

The sea turned to frothy spume. Suddenly the spray falling back to the sea began to turn purple in the fading light.

The whale fought for its last breath while the relent-less catcher slowed its engines. Steadily the winch

reeled the line in. This time the rope tightened, short-
ened, and drew in the whale.

The whale was still struggling, but very feebly. Now
it had to stay on the surface to get enough oxygen into
its dying lungs. The crew gathered expectantly at the
starboard railing.

They yelled and clapped their hands and struck each
other on the back like spectators at a sports show. And
Erik suddenly heard himself shouting and laughing with
the rest. He danced around and around the gunner's
deck with Bornak, waving his arms.

Bornak signaled for more speed. The winch rattled
faster. They were so close to the whale now that Erik
saw its long broad back laboring painfully and slowly
through the slopes of the sea.

Bornak aimed the harpoon barrel down. Again he
squeezed the trigger.

This time no nylon leader line coiled out after the
harpoon. The whale was already hooked. This harpoon
was just a bomb to finish off the animal as quickly as
possible.

The six-foot haft sank deep toward the whale's stubborn heart. It went in just below and in back of the
dorsal fin. Three counts later Erik heard the dreadful
muffled *booommmmm* of the bomb exploding inside
the whale.

Even then the creature summoned enough of its remaining life-force to make one more desperate effort

to escape. It heaved up its weight wearily and sounded.

Bornak's face twisted with rage. The crew swore and stomped the deck with their brass-studded boots.

"Load, load!" Bornak snarled at Erik, and half flung him toward the muzzle of the gun. Erik stumbled, caught himself, then knelt and managed to push another charge and another harpoon into the barrel.

The catcher moved closer to the gasping beast. More bomb fragments tore through its body. Still, somehow, it pulled the catcher a few more hundred yards.

"Half speed astern," Bornak ordered. The catcher pulled backward against the last struggle of the finner. "This is the end, stupid fish." Bornak squeezed the trigger a third time.

Slowly Erik realized that the misty exhalations from the whale were turning pink. The air everywhere around the catcher sparkled with tinted spray.

"She's a-flowering," Bornak shouted with joy.

"Aye," the crew echoed. "She's a-flowering."

Erik had heard the term before and read about it. Now he knew what it meant. It meant that the whale's shattered heart and lungs had finally exploded. The spout was turning pink. It was filling the air with blood.

And that's what flowering is, Erik thought. That's what it means. That's how it looks. The whole world turns all sorts of pretty colors. The sea itself turns red for yards around, and in the red sea the whale rolls over and dies.

The sky trembled dizzily above Erik's head. He couldn't seem to get enough air into his lungs. He struggled to stand there as if nothing were wrong, while Bornak's relentless voice shouted, "Winch him in, Mc-Dun. Fast now. We've got to blast the little one."

SIXTEEN

The smaller whale spouted off the larboard.

"Load, load," Bornak ordered.

Erik swayed uncertainly. Something in his stomach seemed to be going round and round, and the gun up in the triangle of the bows appeared a long way off and fixed at an odd angle as if it were broken.

"Load! What are you waiting for?"

Erik wanted to speak up boldly and honestly, tell Bornak the truth. I'm no good at this business, Bornak, he wanted to say. Being born the son of a gunner king doesn't seem to have made a gunner of me, sir. If it's all the same with you, sir, I want out—out of the whole business—

He shook his head against his own thoughts. That would be ridiculous. He didn't really mean it, and even if it were true, he would never come out and admit such a shameful truth—especially not to Bornak.

Just keep going, he told himself angrily. It's the same as the butcher's deck. Just hang on and you'll get used to this—you can get used to anything, as Old Kra said.

He forced himself ahead until he touched the gun. With a great effort of will, he moved around and dropped on one knee. He got his hands around another iron bomb, lifted it, moved it in toward the head of the loaded harpoon.

The winch rumbled. Its drum reeled in hundreds of feet of dripping line. The whale's white flaccid belly turned up to the sky as it was dragged in and chained alongside the catcher's starboard length.

"Move," Bornak commanded impatiently. "Get it buoyed, away. So we can snag the little one." He slapped Erik on the back. "See, he does as I say. The little tiddler doesn't run. He hangs around worried about what's happened to his father. We have to show him, yah?"

Bornak stamped across to the aft railing of the gun platform. "Tiburon, get some more leader line up here. What are you waiting for?"

Tiburon raised his head above the level of the gun platform. "Why waste our time any longer here, Captain?"

"What's that?" Bornak said, surprised.

"We're supposed to be going for a fortune in fat blues," Tiburon said. "What's the point of taking time to run down a tiddler worth no more than twenty or so barrels of oil? We're losing a lot of time and money here—and anyway, Captain, didn't we learn anything overkilling blues? Do we kill female finners and young finners until there aren't any finbacks left to hunt either? Is that what you want?"

"I want whale, that's what I want, Tiburon. And there'll always be whale for a hunter who is smart enough to get them."

"All right. If you have to kill short whale, Captain, why now? One big blue would be better than ten of these little finners."

"Aye, aye," several of the crew mumbled behind Bornak.

"Thorder, Sigrid," Bornak roared. "Get that leader up here, at once! The rest of you start working on that whale. You're wasting time, all of you. Bornak has never passed up a whale, and he has never cut a line. I've promised you enough blues so that you can retire at the end of the season. If you retire rich men, what do you care if there are not enough whales to go around next year, eh?"

He raised his hands above his head and turned them into fists. Several of the crew began to cheer and laugh.

"When will we be killing big blues, Captain?" Mc-Dun asked.

"Soon, very soon now, we'll be shooting big blues like pigs in a pen. You'll all be millionaires."

"Aye, aye," several crewmen shouted at once.

Tiburon shrugged, glanced at Erik, shook his head quickly twice, and backed out of sight.

Erik went on loading and preparing the gun. Thorder and Sigrid ran to the coils and swung the wet nylon leader up to Bornak. Bornak heaved all two hundred pounds of it up with ease in one hand, flung it to one side, threw an end of it to Erik to lock into the harpoon head. "You look a bit green around the gills, Erik."

Erik shook his head but avoided Bornak's probing gaze. "Just a little seasick maybe," he whispered. "Not used to small boats."

"I know how you feel," Bornak reassured him, grinning broadly. "It happens to the best of gunners, first time on a gunner's deck. You're no softer than any other apprentice, I assure you. Just remember, stick to your gun. Stick to it no matter what, understand? You'll get hardened to it and take it easily in your stride. Why soon enough, lad, you'll be knocking over whale as easily as some landlubbers knock over rabbits."

"Yes, sir," Erik mumbled. He looked at the deck. "Thank you, sir. I'll be all right—"

Erik stood up straight. Learning from the master was a rare opportunity. As Bornak had said, serving his apprenticeship with the king of gunners would make him a famous harpooner. On top of that, he would share with Bornak the greatest of all hunts, the discovery and invasion of the hidden sea of the great blues!

Just look and listen and pay the closest attention,

Erik told himself, and the master will teach you his finest secret skills, all the tricks of the trade.

The crew secured the finback alongside the catcher with more chains. Thorder made a hole in the carcass with a blubber knife. Tiburon and Sigrid unreeled an air hose. A lance-shaped pipe was attached to the end of the hose and pushed into the hole that Thorder had cut. The pump then pressed air into the whale's body as though a balloon were being inflated. Now when it was released by the catcher, the whale would be buoyant enough to float until it was picked up by a corvette and towed away to the factory ship.

Next the crewmen chopped off the dead whale's flukes with axes. This would prevent a strong wind and sea from tearing away the entire tail as the whale drifted. When the flukes were chopped clear, Thorder hacked a long, deep, single notch in the tail's stump to mark the prize as belonging to *Catcher One*.

Sigrid then jammed a fifteen-foot pole into the whale. It flew a black pennant that could be seen at a distance and would help guide in buoy boats and corvettes for the pickup.

Borgen, the radioman, scurried down to the whale from his shack just beneath the bridge. He moved like a nervous terrier, carrying a black metal box with antenna attached to it. He pushed a shaft into the whale's belly. He fixed a short line to it. The other end of the line was fastened to a buoylike object to which the metal box was secured. The buoy then dropped into the sea. This floating transmitter would send out constant code signals. Buoy boats and corvettes could home in on the whale now even in zero visibility, and pickup would be assured despite storms and heavy fogs.

"Pull that hose out now!" Bornak commanded angrily. "How many times do I have to tell you dunderheads that too much air in that carcass can spoil the oil?"

Tiburon yanked out the hose, tossed it onto the foredeck. Thorder and Sigrid jumped onto the carcass. They went over it fore and aft. They trod its flesh with spiked boots as they looked for wounds in the blubber, where fragments of bursting bombs had torn through. Finding such holes, they stuffed them with engine waste and oakum to prevent the pumped-in air from leaking out.

The chains were then unhitched. The carcass drifted away to starboard, its radio-sending buoy bobbing alongside.

Erik watched it go. And in the shadows cast by the drifting icebergs, he saw a strangely disturbing thing. Schools of dolphins leaped around and around the drifting carcass. They seemed to have a kind of mourning concern for their giant lost brother. They kept circling the carcass, nudging and nosing it as though trying to help it out of a mysterious difficulty.

140

Then the whale and the dolphins drifted out of sight and away among the icebergs.

Erik tried to stop thinking about that dead finner and how it had fought so hard to live. . . .

A few moments later Bornak grabbed Erik's arm. He was grinning and pointing to starboard. Half a mile away, the smaller whale was feathering the air with its spout. It was circling the dead whale, nosing in closer and closer. It paid no attention to the approaching catcher.

"See," Bornak said, "how he sniffs around trying to find out what's wrong. Why doesn't daddy swim and play?" He patted the gun's breech. "Soon we'll have more oil, another notch in our gun, eh?"

"Yes, sir," Erik said, looking far to starboard at the clean white sweep of the ice floes.

Bornak swung Erik around and looked at him with a squint of worry. "Every little bit of whale counts. That's Bornak's way. Every little extra barrel of oil counts. Every dead whale adds to a gunner's bonus, regardless of size. There'll always be whale for a good hunter, understand?"

"Yes, sir."

"If you see a female whale with calf, or a short whale, kill it. If you don't, someone else will. Someone else will get the bonus, the money, and the fame."

"Yes, sir."

Bornak released Erik and headed for the harpoon gun. Then he turned, squinted through the spume, and called for "slow to half speed." He swung his left arm backward and forward along the line of the catcher's course, directing the helmsman to steer in that direction and keep a straight line.

"Slow. Slower now. Coast her in now. . . ."

The engine idled down as the catcher crept to within thirty feet of the dead whale. The small finner still nosed and circled it. Thirty feet seemed near enough to give a sporting chance to the baby whale, but Bornak wasn't close enough yet—not for a sure shot. Bornak evidently always wanted a sure shot.

"Sound, sound you crazy little fish!"

The small whale sounded. Bornak directed the catcher straight in toward the dead one. The dolphins fled, leaping over each other, and disappeared among the icebergs.

The small whale broached almost beneath the catcher's bow. It came up spouting less than fifteen feet from Erik, who could follow the scar patterns along its sides and see its eye blinking with puzzled fear.

The small finner swam in and rubbed against the dead whale. It swam away a short distance, then leaped out of the water as if it were trying to argue the big whale into playing leapfrog again.

"Fire," Erik whispered before he could stop himself. "Get it over with."

Bornak jerked around and looked at him questioningly. "I tell you not to go soft, Egil's son. Don't go soft. You'll never be a hunter if you let your heart turn to mush. Whales are fish, you hear. No matter what others say, no matter what you read that your father wrote, whales are nothing but big stupid fish!"

"Yes, sir."

"Big cold fish without feelings."

"Yes, sir."

Bornak turned back to the gun. Erik felt his mouth twitching as the gun roared.

He watched the coils of yellow leader fly out. When he looked up, he saw the harpoon bury itself in the whale's back near the dorsal fin.

Then came the second *booommmmm* of the bomb as it shattered and tore through the inside of the whale.

SEVENTEEN

Four days passed, and on each day as the catcher steamed in the general direction of the Enderby Quadrant, there were whale sightings.

Erik steeled himself to stand beside Bornak. He steeled himself to load the bombs into the harpoons until his hands stopped shaking. He forced himself to stay with Bornak and listen to the bombs go off and watch the whales die. Each time he listened and watched, it was easier to do. The struggles of the whales and the blowing of blood meant less and less. His eyes dulled and his heart grew harder with each killing.

So Old Kra and Bornak were right, Erik decided. You can get used to anything, even killing, if you just stick with it.

Deciphering the code was difficult. He had to sweat out every word and sentence with painful slowness. But translating it was also a great comfort. When he was alone down there, he forgot all about the gunner's deck. Sometimes he wasn't on Bornak's catcher at all, nor in the present time. He was with his father on *Catcher Two*, and it was last year, and he was sharing his father's great discovery of the hidden sea of the blue whales.

His excitement grew as he dug sense out of the code, word by word and sentence by sentence. There were two pages telling how Egil had harpooned a big blue. The blue had dragged the catcher for ten hours, deep into the dangerous ice floes of the Enderby Quadrant. They were near an area Egil had intended to explore in his continuing search for the hidden sea. After they had harpooned the big blue, flagged it, and cast it adrift, Egil had seen the river of krill.

"A strange sight suddenly appeared before our bow," Egil had written in his log. And Erik could imagine the gray-white river, warm and over a hundred yards wide, that he had seen flowing through the green sea. There were billions of shrimp moving with this warm current, a great ocean current of whale food extending far away into the ice floes.

"I shall follow this ocean river as far as I can. It may be that warm current I have been looking for—the one that may lead to the hidden sea that makes up the feeding and breeding ground of the blue whales. . . ."

There followed an account of several days of sailing

this ocean current of krill south-south-by-east until they approached the great, thousand-foot cliffs of the ice barrier.

Later entries in the log read:

"APRIL 12. I have found that legendary sea! My theory was right. The warm river of krill leads straight through the ice mountains that form the northern escarpment of the ice continent.

"The warm current cuts right through the ice barrier like a hot knife through butter. It forms a channel, the only way in to the hidden sea for any sort of ocean-going vessel. Ice walls on either side of the channel rise up several hundred feet straight up like the walls of a fjord.

"The sight of the whales was so awesome that I still feel stunned by the spectacle. Great blues by the thousands were swarming through the ice channel. Thousands of great whales, packed together like sardines, were moving in and out of their hidden sea. The ordinary-sized blue is big enough, up to 120 feet and 140 tons. There were many of these, but here I saw the great granddaddies of all the blues. I saw whales 150 or 170 feet long and weighing up to 200 tons! And, of course, there were swarms of other whales of all sizes: bulls, cows, calves. They were all feeding on the river of krill.

"Needless to say, my catcher crew went wild with joy.

Here was hunting that would make all of us rich men in one short season. A few of these giant 200-ton whales would make us rich, and here were countless numbers of them. We could kill them as fast as we could shoot. We could tally up a bigger bonus, get more oil here in a few weeks than we could ordinarily get in several seasons.

"But the Enderby Quadrant doesn't cooperate with visitors. It is never friendly. It has the most deadly and unpredictable of all seas, and its winds are the coldest and most fierce. The weather changes with sudden violence from warm to freezing and back to warm again. It is a terrible, freakish place where you can never tell what will happen, or how, or when.

"In any case, as we started to move in and begin shooting, we were hit by a ninety-mile-an-hour wind that struck like a thunderclap. The temperature dropped at once to thirty below zero, and continued dropping as we ran for our lives. The sea itself began to freeze around us. We barely escaped toward the Scotia Sea and warmer waters . . . ."

"APRIL 25. The warm current of krill and the channel have disappeared. There is no sign of the whales.

"I put down the exact position of the channel, and we have returned to it. There is nothing here but empty sea, ice, and the broken walls of the ice mountains. Everything is frozen solid.

"There are several possible explanations. The most likely is that the warm current changes its course seasonally, or perhaps vanishes altogether. The current may simply stop flowing from the Indian Ocean at certain times, at regular or irregular intervals, and for unknown periods. The whales may have another way in and out of their hidden sea, under the ice. Or they may wait in the sea until the warm current returns with krill, and with the heat to thaw and cut that channel out again through the ice barrier.

"Anyway, the channel is gone for the present. Needless to say, the crew is disappointed and angry, especially at the Enderby Sea. But there is nothing we can do but sail back toward the Scotia Sea. We must go on hunting what whale we can find. These waters are too dangerous, and we can't waste time. We must hunt whale.

"I've promised the crew we will come back again and look for the hidden sea. Yet I wonder if I want very badly to keep that promise?

"Am I really as disappointed as my crew at finding the channel lost? Am I disappointed at all about not finding the hidden sea? Or am I relieved?

"I've had sober second thoughts about the blue whales. The fleet that invaded their hiding place would become rich and famous in a single season. But it would also be responsible for the extermination of the blues.

"The whales have been mercilessly slaughtered. The

148

hidden sea is their last refuge: it represents their final attempt to save themselves from being wiped out. If this last hiding place in this last corner of the world is invaded, it will mean the end of the great blues, the end of an entire species of life—one of the most ancient forms of life—and the largest that ever lived on this earth.

"Do I want to be responsible for such a thing? I doubt it, but I'm not sure. Maybe I'll come back and lead my men to the channel sea. Maybe I never will.

"Whatever I decide, only I know where it is. I shall put the location down here, as well as this entire account of the hidden sea, in Nordahl code.

"I have told my chief bosun, Gunnar Thorhall, that the location of the channel is here in this logbook, but I haven't told Thorhall what its position is. No one knows that but me. If something should happen to me, Thorhall can decide whether to get its position from this logbook, and to do that he will have to have it decoded by my son, Erik, the only other person in the world who can decipher Nordahl code."

There were a few other brief entries in the log. They were routine notations about the sighting and pursuit of whales, and were not even in code.

Erik didn't bother with them. There was no need to read further. Erik had found what he and Bornak wanted. There it was, decoded and written neatly down on a square of tablet paper.

Run to Bornak with the good news, he thought. Bornak was impatient and eager to know the position and set a course to the hidden sea. He had kept after Erik to hurry—hurry with the code.

Now he'll be happy, Erik thought. He'll be as happy as a bear in a honeypot when I show him the coordinates.

Erik imagined Bornak's booming laughter. Bornak would probably dance a jig, wave his big hands about, and slap Erik on the back. He'll be pleased all right, Erik thought. And Erik had never forgotten how crucially important it was to please Bornak.

Bornak was his patron. Erik's entire future depended on him. Only Bornak could decide when and where Erik got his ten contract shots, whether he was qualified to serve as a gunner, if and when he received his certification, and what rating he would get.

But he didn't move. He just sat at the table, bending over the logbook and his scattered notes. He sat that way, feeling strangely blank and fearful, for what seemed a long time.

He found himself rereading the decoded entries and thinking about what his father had written. The right or the wrong in the possible extermination of the blue whales . . .

Erik read until the words blurred and ran together:

"... *I've a strong suspicion that I can never be responsible for exterminating the last of the great blue whales.*"

Why does everything have to depend on me? Why do I have to end up holding the key to the hidden sea? He struck the tabletop with the flat of his hand so hard that the logbook slid off onto the floor and his notes fluttered through the air.

At that moment he hated his father for putting him in such a position. Egil had decided it was a terrible choice to make, then left it to Erik.

He grabbed up his notes and started toward the compartment door. No true gunner, he thought, would find the location of the hidden sea that was the dream of all great hunters, then turn his back on it and forget about it. No true gunner would worry about killing a few more thousand blues. It didn't worry Bornak, and it wouldn't worry anyone else, Erik thought.

I'm with Bornak, the king of gunners. I'm going to be a gunner, and gunners hunt and kill whales. And as Bornak had said, it doesn't matter how many or what kind of whale—a gunner brings them in, one way or another.

Bornak's hands were unsteady as he looked at the paper Erik had given him. His voice was shaky as he read the position aloud, "Twenty-five degrees west . . . fifty-nine degrees south . . ."

Then he gave out an approving roar of laughter. He

hit Erik across the back. He paced back and forth in his tiny cabin reading the position aloud over and over. Then he pulled dusty maps and charts from a cabinet. He spread the one he wanted across the top of the chart table.

"Twenty-five degrees west . . . fifty-nine degrees south. There she is, Erik." He worked over the chart with calipers and a T square. "There—there's our course. Straight into the heart of the Enderby Quadrant. And into the heart of all the blues left in the world. We'll have our pick, Erik. All we want of the fattest and biggest blues that ever lived."

Erik swallowed painfully. The palms of his hands were wet.

Bornak turned and gripped his shoulder. "You kept your promise, Egil's son. You came through in a great way for Bornak. Now I'll give you your whales, Erik, your ten contract shots. All the whales you want. But you must make your first kill. And your first kill is always the biggest, no matter how many you make later on."

Bornak nodded and grinned, and his big yellow-grained teeth gleamed. "The next one we sight, Erik —it is all yours."

EIGHTEEN

"Hvalblast!"

The cry came out of the Tannoy speaker and ran through Erik like an electric shock. Over ten hours had passed, and they were steaming deeper into the Enderby Sea. Now Erik would have his first great chance at a whale.

He hesitated a moment by the catwalk and sucked gratefully at the icy air.

"Hvalblast!"

The lookout was shouting and waving his arms from the crow's nest, fifty feet above the main deck. He pointed off the port bow. Erik nodded and ran down the catwalk to the bow platform.

Several crewmen on the foredeck were scanning the ocean with binoculars supported by a stick held at waist level. Others, including Bornak, Tiburon, and old Schulstock on the bridge, were watching Erik solemnly.

Then Tiburon ran down the catwalk and helped Erik lift the 160-pound harpoon and slam it into the barrel. "You've been busy. I haven't had a chance to return these," Tiburon said.

Erik took the wallet and the ring. He put the wallet in his jacket. He stared at the ring a moment with its thick gold band and its ruby stone shaped like a finwhale. He had almost forgotten it and the inscription inside its band. For an uneasy moment, he wondered why he could have forgotten something that meant so much:

"To my son, Erik, Prince of Gunners—and one day a king."

He felt a twinge of confusion and loss, then he shrugged and turned his eyes stubbornly toward the sea where a slate-gray ocean joined a lead-gray sky.

"Good luck, kid." Tiburon leaped the railing and disappeared below.

Erik took a slow, deep breath and squinted back to port, searching for the spout of his whale.

A light rain fell, but the wind lashed it into Erik's face like buckshot. It penetrated his sou'wester and ran over his skin in icy driblets. Icebergs several miles long drifted against the gray horizon. Many smaller bergy chunks dotted the surrounding sea. Ice clutter, Erik thought with a thrum of warning. It was bad stuff for a catcher to plunge through during a fast chase.

He shivered a little and glanced skyward. Blue petrels skimmed the air. Just above the crow's nest soared three wandering albatross. They moved effortlessly, in supreme control of the wind, seeming never to flap their twelve-foot wings. From a drifting iceberg came the piteous wailing sound of seal pups. It was startlingly like the cries of lost children.

"*Hvalblast!*"

"Where?" Erik called up to the lookout. "Where now?"

The lookout pointed two points off the port bow.

Erik strained his eyes. Walls of ice glowed from the southern fringe of the pack ice as a line of mist cleared away.

Erik hesitated, then reached back nervously, and pulled the engine-room telegraph handle to "full speed." He gave proper hand and arm signals to the helmsman.

The catcher responded at once to his command, heeling obediently to port like a trained hound. He knew what he was doing. His father had made him rehearse over and over everything that could happen on a gunner's deck. Egil had coached him through every possible situation until he was sure Erik could act fast, without thinking.

Erik had also read everything he could find on the subject. He had watched Bornak, and memorized his every word. But now his hands were wet inside his gloves. His chest felt heavy. His confidence wavered as he saw himself completely alone, and fully responsible, on the gunner's deck. Then he smiled a little as he braced hard into the wind.

"Where now?" he shouted.

"Straight ahead," answered the lookout.

"Steady as she goes," Erik said.

McDun jumped behind the foredeck winch. Erik balanced himself as the catcher shuddered and slammed into a big sea. Clouds of white water burst up from her bows and washed over the decks. Now and then came the threatening rasp of ice chunks scraping along the hull.

The ice cluster was bad and would probably get worse, Erik reasoned. But Shelties were the best sailors in the world, and Schulstock would have to be one of the best even among Shelties, or Bornak would never have chosen him as helmsman.

Erik bent down to grip the iron bomb in both hands. In his excitement he had forgotten what that bomb had meant to him earlier. Anyway, he told himself, those qualms and fears are all over for me.

But as he started to rise and slam the bomb into the harpoon, his body seemed anchored to the deck by invisible ropes. He felt dizzy, and the gun a few inches from his face blurred. He gritted his teeth. He felt his face turning rigid with strain.

Then he was free. He jumped up with the bomb and

stumbled only a little as he pushed it into the harpoon and twisted it in solid. Then he moved faster and more freely as he checked the halyards and hooked in the leader line.

Looking over to port then, he saw the spout.

For a long moment he forgot to breathe. He studied it carefully and there was no mistaking its design.

It was the spout of a big blue.

"Blaahval! Blaahval!"

The lookout waved his hands wildly and took up the cry: *"Blaahval!"*

Any blue whale was a prize catch. When they were plentiful, no other whale was hunted. One big blue was equal to several smaller species. That was the reason they had been hunted to the point of extinction. But Erik sensed that this whale meant more to everyone than just a bigger bonus and more oil in the factory tanks.

To the whalemen it was the first big blue of the season. Maybe to them it meant the beginning of all the many blues that Bornak had promised them.

And it was Erik's first kill. It was his first, and as Bornak had said, it would always be the biggest of his life. His hands trembled a little as he checked the gun breech load. Right and ready. Everything was ready.

"Full speed ahead," he called down the phone. He

tried to make his voice low and powerful in his throat, but it didn't sound the least like Bornak's.

He gripped the harpoon gun. The catcher crept in fast toward the position of the whale. His nerves felt like coiled springs.

The blue sped through the rough sea like a huge torpedo. It spouted at regular intervals of about sixteen seconds, and made short, quick sounds, coming up again and blowing and rolling playfully about.

Erik studied its antics with a growing suspicion that something was wrong.

The whale's movements weren't right. It was behaving strangely.

Finners were fast, elusive. The blues tended to sound for longer periods and come up far off course. They usually required longer, more careful stalkings than finners.

But this blue wasn't acting like a blue. It must be a blue because it wasn't behaving like a finner either, and besides its spout was definitely a blue's. But it wasn't acting like any whale was supposed to act. It was moving too much on the surface and in too steady and straight a line for a blue. Its sounds were too short and quick.

"New course on the whale's track," he called up to the helmsman. "Fall off a point."

"Aye."

"*Hvalblast,*" said the lookout, pointing.

"Do we gain much?" Erik asked nervously.

"Two hundred yards."

He felt the steady, critical eyes of Bornak and the others on him as he turned and peered uncertainly into the spray. The spout shot up with a roar, and Erik pulled the engine-room telegraph handle again to full speed. An enormous shadow filled the sea. The great blue was suddenly no more than a hundred feet away.

The range closed: ninety feet, sixty feet, fifty feet.

A great grayish-blue and black body projected itself out of the sea just ahead. Up and up until fifty feet or more were clear of the water. The whale seemed to hang suspended for an instant, and then it fell back in a welter of spray and foam. A moment later there was a second leap, and the animal's great head was silhouetted against the sky. Erik heard a loud *woosh* and a drone that sounded like air rushing into a huge cavern.

Then the whole of that vast 110-foot body was there before him. Massive yet apparently weightless, the whale swam along with ponderous majesty. Its movements seemed nearly effortless. Its huge flukes swung lazily up and down and twisted in a kind of rotary motion.

The giant beast did not seem frightened. It seemed to radiate friendliness. As it rolled over in the sea, Erik saw the long pleated furrows of its belly and throat sweeping up to a curved, almost smiling mouth and those merry, tear-shaped wrinkles of skin surrounding the tiny eyes.

Something about its great size and the surrounding wilderness of sea and ice seemed about to crush Erik. He felt as though his courage, his sense of importance, were being shriveled down to nothing in the wind.

But it was a blue whale. No doubt about that now, not at this close range. Still, it acted strangely unlike a blue.

Erik called down for half speed. The catcher slid in closer, and Erik wondered uneasily why the whale didn't broach. It has to broach for a sure shot. Bornak had taught him that. It had to broach, so he could get in close enough for that sure shot.

"A hundred-and-twenty barrels of oil," yelled a voice from the foredeck. "Or I've never seen a whale!"

"Blast its heart out, lad," pleaded McDun.

"Bornak," another voice begged, "take this one yourself. Don't let that greenhorn kid risk losing a big one."

"Aye, aye," agreed someone else. "Let the kid work out on a tiddler. We need that big fish."

Erik's face burned with shame and resentment. He glanced up at Bornak on the bridge. Bornak, smiling reassurance, slowly shook his head.

Erik turned back with relief toward the gun. Why should Bornak worry? He knew that a fortune in blues waited just ahead in the hidden sea.

They want this big blue desperately, Erik thought, and I've got to give it to them—to them, and to myself.

But he studied the whale with deepening concern. It refused to make the customary deep broach. It swam on the surface in a sluggish crooked crawl, again about a hundred feet in front of the catcher. It should have sounded minutes ago with a boat so near.

Even when the catcher moved in close, the blue did not sound. It made several quick shallow dives. It scooped up in its jaws a few thousand krill now and then. It wouldn't sound.

Erik began to wonder if there could be such a thing as a crazy whale.

Then he stopped wondering. Suddenly he knew that the whale was not really acting strangely at all.

When the whale altered course slightly, Erik saw clearly what swam alongside it. A baby whale. The big blue was a mother whale, and the baby swam steadily along behind the mother's dorsal fin.

Not crazy then. Not even strange. Just unfamiliar. Erik had never seen such a sight, nor been taught how mother whales behaved with baby whales.

Erik wiped spray from his eyes and called for lower speed. Now as the catcher coasted in, Erik saw the baby quite clearly. He remembered a few facts he'd read about them. And he knew they weigh about two tons at birth and are about twenty-four feet in length. But for all of its size, a baby whale is as limp and uncoordinated as a baby calf. The mother nurses her baby, like any other mammal, and often carries it on her back or in her mouth.

This baby whale was probably a day or two old, at least. Compared to the mother, it was still a tiny creature. Since birth it had been growing at the rate of ten pounds an hour, and it could swim rather well now. It still acted and looked like a baby.

It swam closer to its mother, hugging her side.

Erik stared and kept wiping spray from his eyes with the back of his gloves. He remembered Old Kra saying that the most important whaling law was the one against killing a mother whale with calf.

A baby whale had no chance for survival when its mother was dead. It would never grow up and help preserve a doomed species. Instead, it would swim about helplessly looking for its dead mother. It would soon starve to death or be eaten by sea leopards.

Erik turned hopefully toward the bridge and looked up at Bornak, but the giant stood as before, his head nodding, his teeth shining in that reassuring grin.

Erik looked down at the foredeck. The crew continued their preparations for the kill. Still hoping, driven by a kind of desperate panic, Erik looked up at Bornak again, then at the crew, at Schulstock, back at Bornak.

But they didn't care about the mother whale with calf. They were only concerned about the bonus and the oil, and about whether or not Erik could prove himself as a whale killer. They had never cared about the whaling laws or what they killed, Erik thought. Probably no whalemen had ever cared. If they had, there wouldn't be a shortage of whales.

So if whalemen have never worried, Erik thought, why should I?

NINETEEN

He crouched and peered ahead along the up-angled barrel of the harpoon gun.

Bornak had said to kill any whale that swims. He ought to know. He was the all-time king of gunners. Bornak had said to kill whatever you got in your sights and make your bonus, because if you didn't do it, someone else would.

And Bornak had said it was all a lot of nonsense anyway, this so-called critical shortage of whale. There would always be whale for a gunner good enough to find and kill them.

But it wasn't easy to keep watching the whales, to keep leaning on the gun breech, testing the sight, going over the proper ways to shoot.

There was always the baby whale swimming along by its mother's side. It was an exact miniature of her. It swam hard, sending its tiny spout up only a few feet several times a minute.

It was clear enough now why the mother had refused to sound or increase her speed. Erik thought of the things he'd read about dolphins and about how the other smaller whale had been so reluctant to leave its father. Whale were the giant brothers of the dolphin with the same strong sense of loyalty to their family. Adult dolphins do not abandon their young. Neither do whales, thought Erik. The mother blue hasn't considered sounding and swimming away from the calf. She has had to hold her pace down to that of the baby's top speed. Now it was struggling beside her, panting hard to keep up, inhaling and exhaling with all of its might.

Erik stared through a fog of numbing confusion. He bent stiffly over the gun. He felt that peculiar miserable ache in his stomach. His nerves seemed to be concentrated in the tips of his fingers, around his mouth, and along the bridge of his nose.

The ultrasonic vibrations went out. At once the blue whale broke her pattern. She picked up speed, spurted ahead—but still refused to leave the baby whale. She folded it under her right dorsal fin. Holding it firmly, she beat her powerful flukes and pulled away from the catcher.

Erik saw that she was trying to keep the baby whale's head out of the water so it wouldn't drown, trying to escape the catcher and at the same time let the small one keep on breathing.

Erik squeezed a shout from his throat. He called down into the engine room: "Full speed ahead."

The catcher lunged, gaining rapidly on the blue, driving its hull through the swells at seventeen knots. The whale rolled and arched through the air. Still gripping the baby at her side, she submerged.

Erik flung himself to the deck. The feel of the icy black deck plates bit through his clothes and seemed to numb his flesh. He lay flat and peered over the gunwale. The whale had made only a shallow sound, he knew. Then he saw her immense shadow down a few fathoms. This was a trick his father had taught him— to lie this way on the deck and follow the underwater path of a whale, and at the same time guide the catcher by means of hand signals to the helmsman.

He strained his eyes down through a bubbling green. More to starboard, he waved. There a little more. That's it . . . Steady now . . . steady as she goes now. . . .

He leaped to his feet and to the phone. "Stop engines. Hold her down now."

He reached out and touched the pistol grip. He swung the gun hard to starboard.

The whale will have to surface quickly, he thought, waiting for her to broach. The baby whale will need air now. It can't stay under nearly as long as the big whale.

Yes, she was coming up already, less than ten feet from the catcher's larboard.

166

He stumbled at the gun. That strangely blank and fearful numbness seized him again. He seemed to be taken over and moved by some power outside of himself, some other will that was not his own.

He saw his arms moving, but they seemed to belong to someone else. He had no brain or will of his own. Something had to be done. He was doing it—he had to do it—but somehow it was not really him—

The arms and the hands raised the angle of the barrel. They shifted the angle a bit higher, then moved the gun to the right, then a bit to the left—

Then Erik was crouching lower and squinting hard down the length of the barrel. He was aiming with slow deliberate care.

He was doing the aiming now. His hands were moving the gun barrel. He felt responsible again, but he didn't know whether he should congratulate himself or not.

There was a sharp explosion less than ten feet from the bow. Fifty feet of mist spread over the gunner's deck in a delicate rain. The whale was rising again, higher and higher.

It might have been a weirdly speckled island emerging out of the sea. Great waves caught the catcher and flung it about, bucking and yawing, like a toy boat.

The blue seemed to look at Erik then. She slowly blinked her too big, too intelligent, too human, and too sad eyes.

Erik steadied the gun barrel. He aimed. But there's

really no need to aim, he thought suddenly. The wall of flesh was everywhere. It was too close to miss. It was not the sort of target anyone could miss, unless they turned and fired in the opposite direction.

Anyone can do this, Erik thought. The harpoon will hold. It will go off inside the whale and kill it. If this harpoon doesn't do it, the next one will, or the next. And there are always more harpoons waiting. You can hardly miss hitting the whale at this range. And once you hit it, it must surely die.

Just shoot, he thought. It is easier than shooting pigs in a pen. Yes, how easy it is after all. How easy to kill the biggest thing that ever lived on earth. Just get in close enough and pull a trigger. Prongs, flanges, bombs, shrapnel, a winch, a six-inch line and the pull of a five-hundred-ton catcher would do the rest.

"Why anyone can do it," Erik whispered aloud. "Even a kid—"

"Fire," shouted Bornak at the top of his lungs. "Fire!"

The blue's full length was almost clear of the water. Her churning flukes held her high above the catcher as the baby whale wriggled and snorted under her fin.

"Fire, fire!" Bornak yelled, not louder, but nearer.

Erik was down on one knee behind the gun. He kept trying to sight just back of and below the dorsal fin. At least be as kind about it as you can, he thought. That is supposed to be the merciful place to shoot them.

But the blue was dropping again, dropping down into the sea. It was sinking out of the sky, back down past the line of the starboard railing toward the darkening swirl of the deeps.

She seemed to sink in slow motion, supported by the power of her churning flukes.

"Fire," Bornak's voice was thundering in his head now.

"Fire," Erik whispered at his hands.

First one, then the other, moved around the pistol grip. But neither hand would do what he wanted it to do. Neither one of them would pull the trigger . . .

TWENTY

Erik saw Bornak charging toward him down the catwalk from the bridge. He was waving his fists.

Erik willed his hand to squeeze the trigger. Nothing happened.

Then there was no target. There was no whale to kill. No mother whale, no baby whale. Nothing to see but freezing spray hurling across the sky. Nothing to hear but the wind's moan and the waves pounding on the catcher's hull and on the distant shores of ice.

He was still staring up the angled barrel, but the sights were targeted on an empty sky. Then it wasn't quite empty. Streaks of dark clouds appeared. A wandering albatross drifted through a flurry of mist and a few scattered flakes of snow.

Dry strange snow, Erik thought, a powdery stuff that blew away as soon as it touched the deck and left no trace, like pigeon's feathers.

He aimed at the emptying, then darkening sky for no

more than a second's time. Yet, incredibly, during that second, he had a vision, a kind of daydream so vividly real that he actually saw it.

He saw himself as he had always thought he should and would be. He bore gunner's scars on his hands and face. His beard was stiff with frozen spray and whale blood, and he stood above the giant carcass of the whale he had killed.

He smiled as he strode back up the catwalk to the bridge, and the crew slapped him on the back, and they lifted him to their shoulders and they bore him aloft, high above everyone and everything, above the whale and the sea and the catcher and the world.

He smiled down on them with the smile of a man who has met life's greatest challenge—and won.

But it was only a vision, and in a flash it was gone. Erik knew it was really gone, gone for good. It was a sad thing, he thought. It was as if some very dear friend he had known a long time had suddenly said good-bye . . .

Then Erik felt something else happen. It was too sudden and strange and incredible for him to understand at once what it was. But it was the opposite of being sad.

He was glad. He was glad that he had not shot the whale.

He had no idea why he should feel this way when he had failed, when he had lost his great chance—when

Bornak was running toward him down the catwalk, his face livid and contorted with rage as though Erik had committed the most horrible and traitorous crime.

He felt like laughing and jumping up and running and leaping about the decks like a mad man. He felt suddenly light, light as air, as if he had wings that had been tied and were now unbound. He felt he could take off into the sky as effortlessly as the albatross floating above the masthead.

He ought to feel ashamed and lower than a crawling snake, but he didn't. And underneath his stunned confusion he sensed a new trueness and strength.

Then Bornak was dragging him back, hoisting him aloft with one hand. "This is your whale. What's the matter with you? Shoot it."

Erik shook his head. He started to laugh. Not at Bornak. But at the whole mess, because it seemed so funny—all this hullabaloo over a whale. He choked down the laugh, and shook his head slowly at Bornak.

"I—I don't think so, sir."

"What? What?" roared Bornak.

"You—you can have this whale, sir."

"Are you crazy?"

"No, sir. Well, I don't think so."

"Shut up!" Bornak roared louder.

Erik nodded and shut up.

A voice shrilled up from the foredeck. "Take it, take it, Bornak. She's yours."

"Aye, the kid's turned to mush. Take it, Bornak."

"Blast her heart out, Cap'n."

"Yah, yah," Bornak shouted. Still holding onto Erik the giant turned toward the gun. His eyes gleamed and bulged with a sudden flare of excitement. "Yah, I'll get her for sure, that big stupid fish!" He seemed to forget Erik and hurled him away as he turned and leaped at the harpoon gun.

Erik felt a dull thud explode at the back of his head as he struck the railing, then slammed into the black iron plates of the deck. He rolled, stunned and blinded, a few feet across the gunner's deck, his legs becoming entangled in the coils of yellow nylon leader.

He shook his head and tried to raise himself up onto his arms. He couldn't move. He began to see Bornak's fuzzy outline near the gun.

The whale had broached and surfaced again quickly. "Hold that fat back still, lady," Bornak was pleading as he sighted down over the railing at a sharp angle toward the disappearing back of the whale. "Right there . . . that's it. . . . Steady now, old girl. . . ."

Erik heard a high-pitched shout—he twisted with difficulty and looked toward the foredeck. He saw Tiburon, his face pinched with fear. The bosun was running wildly across the foredeck toward the gun platform, waving his arms and shouting frantically at Erik:

"The line—get clear for God's sake—"

Line? Line?

Tiburon leaped. He grabbed the rim of the gun plat-form and pulled himself up. He shouted at Erik. He turned his face up, white with fear, toward Bornak. He called to Bornak, but the gunner didn't hear him. Bor-nak didn't seem to be aware of anything but the gun and the whale.

The line—suddenly Erik realized his danger. The yel-low nylon leader entangled about his legs. . . . When the harpoon fired—

Erik tore at the nylon coils in a spasm of terror. Tiburon crawled over the rim of the platform and grabbed Erik's arm and pulled at him, but the line lead-ing up to the harpoon head refused to let him go.

Erik struggled to a sitting position, then twisted around and down to where he could get hold of the entangling coils with both hands. He saw that Bornak was about to squeeze the pistol grip. The harpoon would blast away, whipping the nylon line after it. It would catapult Erik out into the sea as it went, and it would drag him on down, after the whale.

Erik tugged frantically at the line, trying to extricate his left leg from the heavy wet trap of the coils. But in that terrible part of a second he knew he could never free himself before Bornak squeezed the trigger.

Tiburon knew it, too. He leaped across the gun deck toward Bornak, shouting with all the force he could summon against the clatter of the winch motor and the howl of the wind:

"Don't shoot, Bornak. The kid's in the line. Don't shoot—"

But if Bornak heard the warning, he gave no sign of it. He was going to fire. Tiburon grabbed his arm with both hands and twisted it away from the trigger.

Even then Bornak did not turn his head away from the whale. He gave out a bellow of irritation, and without looking behind him, he swung out his arm in a powerful backhand smash. The blow caught Tiburon across the side of the head. Erik heard him groan as he struggled to get up.

Erik finally managed to kick his boot free of the nylon coils. He got one leg bent under him, and leaped away from the harpoon line. At that instant the gun exploded. A cloud of black smoke billowed over the deck, and Erik felt the nylon whipping out only a few inches from his ear.

He hugged the deck and heard the half-sobbing sounds coming out of his throat. He didn't trust himself to try to get up onto his feet. Instead he slid back to the far side of the gun platform, near Tiburon and as far from the harpoon gun as he could get.

"Fast fish," Bornak roared. "Fast fish!"

Then, four seconds after the harpoon struck, came the muffled *booommmmm* of the bomb exploding inside the whale.

Tiburon was rubbing the side of his head and wincing a little as his fingers touched a swelling lump. He looked at Erik with a puzzled frown. But there was no mockery in his expression now, and there was a friendliness and a respect that Erik had not seen before.

Tiburon stopped rubbing his head. All the time he studied Erik with that puzzled but respectful curiosity. "Well," he said then. "Why didn't you shoot the whale?"

Erik heard another *booommmmm*. The catcher shook from the recoil. Bornak, with his special skill, had gotten another harpoon into the whale before it could broach. The great flukes beat the sea, and the tail rose over a hundred feet above the catcher.

Erik watched the main whale line, thick as a man's arm, tauten. The rope creaked dangerously where it ran through the bows. Then Erik felt the catcher lunge ahead. The blue whale was unleashing her full power and was towing the ship through the field of drifting icebergs and ice clusters.

"Seems you had everything to gain," Tiburon insisted, his voice sharp with interest. "All you had to do was pull the trigger. You couldn't miss. What did you stand to lose?"

"I don't know," Erik finally said, slowly. "I—I just didn't want to shoot that whale."

"That's a very good reason, I think," Tiburon said.

Then he dropped down out of sight, and Erik heard Bornak's voice shouting for "half speed."

Bornak stayed hunched over the gun, facing into the

driving spray. He had never turned to see what had happened to Erik, and Erik knew that the king of gunners didn't care. He was never my father's friend, or mine, Erik thought. All he wanted from me was the location of the hidden sea.

Erik stayed topside and watched as the blue dragged the catcher through the graying sea. Icebergs and ice clusters flew past the plunging ship.

Then he slipped down from the gun platform and went below to his compartment.

TWENTY-ONE

On the way he ran into several members of the crew. They didn't seem to scorn or ridicule him. They just pretty much ignored him. It was as though he were no longer a part of the crew, let alone a prince of gunners. It was a cramped ship, and it didn't need an extra passenger. He was just excess baggage, and the few members of the crew who showed any feeling for him at all seemed merely to feel sorry for him.

Erik went on to his compartment, and stretched out on his bunk. He didn't turn on the light. He lay down in his wet, half-frozen clothes, and he stared up wearily at the overdeck plates, at the dim shadowed patterns made by the rusted rivet heads.

His new sense of trueness and strength held inside him. No matter what Bornak and the crew thought of him, he still felt good about not shooting the whale. He wasn't confused now about that.

But he also felt a pressing loneliness. As he lay there, eyes aching in the darkness, he felt even more alone than he'd been in his cargo cave on the *Arcturus*.

He wasn't a prince of gunners—at least, not on this ship. He wasn't an apprentice. On this ship, with Bornak as captain, he wasn't anything—at least, not to Bornak or the crew.

But he was here, he reminded himself, and he would have to survive and make the most of it.

Lying there, he felt the terrible cold seeping in through the black hull plates. He could tell by the ship's movements that it was still being pulled at top speed by the whale. Ice scraped and ground along the hull.

He tried to sleep. He kept dozing off and waking up suddenly, shivering. He thought of the catcher being dragged ahead—helpless so long as it stayed hooked to the giant whale.

And to where? Somewhere deeper into the dreaded Enderby Quadrant, the "devil's sea."

Erik sat up suddenly. The thought that seemed to have wakened him lingered in his brain. He stared into the darkness and decided he had to talk with Tiburon.

He found him sitting alone in the dimly lit fo'c'sle. He was hunched over a table and a nearly empty cup of coffee.

"Why would my father have asked Bornak to help me—and be my patron as an apprentice gunner?" Erik asked. "Why—when I know now that my father couldn't have liked Bornak or trusted him?"

Tiburon's mouth twisted down on one side in a sardonic grin. "That's a good question. Why should he? But we'd better not worry so much about the past and where we've been, I'm thinking. We'd better worry about where we're heading. I think we're in for deep trouble, Erik. Bad seas and worse weather."

He stared at the bulkhead a moment, shivered again, then turned his one eye up at Erik. "Bornak's just told us what some of us have suspected all along—that he knows where the hidden sea is, the secret breeding ground of the blue whale. And he's going to invade it. That's where he intends to find all those thousands of blues he promised us. That's how we're all going to get rich this season, killing big blues." Tiburon leaned over and gave a low, painful laugh. "A myth, a legend, a fairy tale."

"You don't believe there's a hidden sea of the blue whale?" Erik said.

"Another crazy whaleman's dream," Tiburon growled. "You might as well believe in Valhalla."

"What about the rest of the crew?" Erik asked. "Do they believe Bornak can find the hidden sea for them?"

Tiburon's old mocking grin came back as he glared up at Erik. "Most of them. They all want to believe that Bornak can make them rich and famous. They've all sworn allegiance to him, for he's the king of gunners, and they've said they'll follow him anywhere."

Erik smiled a little. "I don't know about Valhalla, but there is a hidden sea."

Tiburon's eye blinked slowly. "You know that for a fact? Yes, I wondered if this hunt for the blues had something to do with your father and you. Why else would Bornak go to the trouble of helping you? How's it tied up with you? Through your father? Through Egil?"

Erik nodded. He told Tiburon the story that he'd gotten from Bornak. Egil's catcher dragged into the ice and destroyed by a blue whale. The SOS. Bornak reaching the site of the wreck after the catcher had gone down with all hands except Egil. Before he died, Egil had given the logbook to Bornak and said, according to Bornak, that he was to keep it safe and later share it and the great hunt through the hidden sea with Erik.

"According to that story, my father and Bornak had to have been friends," Erik said. "But I can't now see my father as any friend of Bornak's."

"Why does that story make them seem friendly?"

"Every reference in that logbook to the hidden sea was in Nordahl code. Bornak couldn't read it. That was why he needed me. My father must have told Bornak that the logbook held the location of the hidden sea, or else Bornak would never have known about it. If my father did that, he must have been a friend of Bornak's, and trusted him. But he would have known Bornak too well for that. Or maybe my father was raving—out of his head with pain."

Tiburon shook his head, and then he put his hand flat over his eye patch and squeezed his other eye shut a moment as though he had a headache. "No," he said, his eye still closed. "Bornak lied all the way. And you're right. Bornak hated your father. And your father wouldn't have trusted Bornak any further than he could have thrown a bull sea elephant.

"No. Bornak hated your father, because your father refused to kill illegal whale. Your father believed the laws of the whaling commission should be obeyed, or whale would be wiped out and all whaling would end. Of course, he was right."

Tiburon took another drink of coffee and went on. "Bornak hated your father even more because Egil was organizing whalemen and gunners, trying to get them to obey the whaling laws. Anyway, Erik, he lied about your father's death and the logbook."

"How?" Erik said flatly.

"I was there," Tiburon said. "We answered the SOS all right. When we got there, the catcher had gone down with all hands but one. Only that one was not your father. Egil had also gone down with his ship."

"Then who—"

"It was Egil's first mate, Gunnar Thorhall, whom Bornak found still alive on the ice. He had your father's logbook, and he must have given it to Bornak and told him that Egil had found the hidden sea and that the information about it was in the logbook."

"Yes," Erik whispered. "Thorhall knew that. But my father never told him the location."

"For that," Tiburon said wryly, "Bornak had to have you. You and the code and the hidden sea. That's all he wanted, or cared about you for. Everything else was a lie."

Erik sat down heavily on an adjoining bunk. He looked down at the floor. Finally he said in a low hesitant voice, "Tiburon— Was I right in not killing the mother whale with the calf? Were my father and the whaling commission right about not killing—"

"Sure they're right, and you're right," Tiburon said. "It's stupidly wrong to overkill and wipe out a whole species. Especially if you're dependent on it for food and a hundred other products. It's too bad living things kill each other to eat, but they do.

"Whalemen seem to be an especially greedy, short-sighted lot. They've killed whale faster than whale can breed, so the creatures are nearly extinct. Can you imagine killing off pigs, cows, and sheep faster than they can breed, so that you end up without any pigs, cows, or sheep?"

Erik hesitated. He kept looking down at the black riveted deck plates. "My father didn't think the hidden sea should be hunted. Do you, Tiburon?"

"If there should be a hidden sea, I'd be dead against hunting in it."

"Why?"

"Same reason I'm against killing illegal whale. I'd rather preserve the species and preserve whaling, if I had anything to say about it. If they find that hidden sea, gunners like Bornak'll clean it out."

Erik shook his head, and his voice was very low and tight in his throat. "I don't feel so good, Tiburon. I've been a fool all right."

"Haven't we all?" Tiburon said.

"But if it weren't for me," Erik groaned, "Bornak could never find the secret sea. I am the only one who knows its secret. If it weren't for me, the hidden sea could stay hidden. We wouldn't be risking the ice in Enderby Quadrant, and the last of the blues might survive."

"You didn't know," Tiburon said. "I also trusted Bornak for a long time. Most of the catcher crew believe in him still. So don't blame yourself. Don't blame yourself for wanting and trying to believe that a hero and a king of gunners was not a greedy liar."

"What can we do now?" Erik wondered aloud, not looking at Tiburon. "What can I do? I've given Bornak the location—I can't take that back."

184

"What can we do now?" Tiburon repeated in a very worried tone. "What can anyone do against a gunner captain like Bornak? Bornak has killed too many whale for too long. Since he was nine years old—that was when his father first took him aboard his catcher—since then, for forty years, Bornak has known nothing else but killing whales. He's not likely to turn back, is he? from the hidden sea and his last great hunt."

Erik said nothing. He took a deep breath and stood up and went out of the fo'c'sle and topside to the foredeck. There he stood back out of sight near the superstructure, and he looked out through the snow at Bornak who still stood by the harpoon gun.

The dark wind now hurled snow and needling spicules of ice. In the weird twilight, Bornak stood over his gun like a statue, high on the flaring prow.

The great blue whale still towed the catcher at a steady seventeen knots. It slowed occasionally, then lunged ahead again with undiminished determination.

The crewmen moved about the foredeck shivering in the snow. Their faces were white and drawn with worry.

"Cut the line," McDun pleaded.

"Aye, cut 'er," Thorder shouted hoarsely.

"Cut her, or we'll be in the ice."

Bornak turned slowly like an animated snowman and shook his fists at them. His voice roared through the wind and snow with fierce defiance:

"Bornak's never cut a line. He never will. And if any

of you are afraid to follow the whale, jump into that freezing muck and swim home."

No whaleman after that mentioned cutting the line. It didn't matter very much where the whale dragged the catcher. They were still in the Enderby Quadrant, and when the whale finally died, Bornak would not be too far from the hidden sea.

And he would try to get there, Erik thought. Bornak would have to keep going. Bornak would never give up. Bornak would have to go on to the end of this great hunt, Erik knew, no matter where it took him, or how long. He would have to go on and kill the whales even if he froze and drowned himself and all of his crew.

What could ever stop Bornak now?

TWENTY-TWO

The blue finally gave up and died, but Erik couldn't stop thinking about the baby whale. It had been found still clutched under the mother's dorsal fin. It had been dead from suffocation a long time.

Later, as he started from the galley back to his cabin, he overheard a conversation between Bornak and Borgen, the radioman.

Borgen's voice was a frightened whine as he said, "They're not following us, I tell you, Captain!"

"You told those yellow-bellied pigs we're hunting the hidden sea of blue whales, didn't you?" roared Bornak furiously.

"Yes, sir, but it's useless now," the radioman whined. "None of those other catchers will follow us another mile into this sea."

"You sure they understood that I've found the secret breeding ground of the blues?"

"Yes, sir. I told them. Some of them didn't seem to believe it, sir. Others—well—they won't risk the Enderby—"

"Get back up to your radio," Bornak shouted. "Tell them they'd better believe it. In a few weeks we'll flag enough whale to retire everybody in this fleet for life! We'll have more oil than all the other fleets in *Zuther Notion* put together!"

"I told them," the radioman said wearily.

Erik slipped along the rusted bulkhead until he was able to look through the partly opened door.

"Tell them again," Bornak shouted, his throat swollen with rage.

"It's no use. I can't reach them now in any case."

"Why not?" Bornak shook the smaller man savagely.

"They're out of range, sir. Everyone and everything's out of range in this godforsaken sea. It's the worst area on earth for radio. Just big patches of dead spots."

"What about the *Arcturus*?"

"She's out of the two-hundred-mile range, sir."

"Keep trying. I can't believe those other catchers will really drop out."

"But the last message was from Gunner Captain Trasti, sir."

"Trasti! That spineless rat. What did he say?"

"He said he was taking over command of the catcher fleet, sir. Said they'd taken a vote. Decided not to follow you any further into the Enderby. They dropped out of convoy at five degrees east and fifty-seven degrees south. I don't think there's any way to get in touch with them now, sir, not unless we circle back."

"Circle back!" Bornak's laugh was contemptuous as he shook his head. "We're going on after those big blues."

Erik felt the increasing cold chipping away at his bones. Shivering, he crept below to warm himself.

Hours later an enraged Bornak called Erik up to the bridge. He grabbed a fistful of Erik's sou'wester and pushed him against the railing. "You lied to me!"

Erik twisted free and shook his head. Bornak pointed to port. "This is the position you gave me. Twenty-five west, fifty-nine south. Right?"

"That's right," Erik said.

"But there's no channel. No sea," Bornak growled. "Nothing."

Erik looked. His body seemed to shrink from the immensity of the spectacle rising above and away to the far horizon. The icy sky had cleared to a vast blue arch, crossed with the flares of the southern lights. It was one great path of tracery, faint white, laced with brilliant reds and greens and blues.

Under that colossal sky the horizon was a pattern of drifting icebergs: gigantic bergs many miles long and hundreds of feet high. Reaching away to east and west as far as Erik could see was the great wall of the floating ice continent—a cragged and towering barrier of ice.

"I've cruised up and down this ice wall for hours," Bornak said. "The ice is solid, and there is no channel opening anywhere. There is no sign of a break in the freeze, and yet we are right here where you tell me the sea is."

Erik looked down into the sea to port, then to starboard. He stared into the mysterious depths that seemed to crawl with silent, enormous shadows. Giant strands of rust-red kelp drifted by, twenty feet long and thicker than a man's body. The strands undulated and twisted like nests of sea serpents. It was the devil's sea all right, surrounded by a great white and silent wilderness of snow and ice—

And with no gray-white river of krill. Erik searched carefully over the sea's surface in all directions. There was no sign of the krill current that his father had followed to the ice barrier. ". . . the warm current cuts right through the ice barrier, like a hot knife through butter," his father had written. "It forms a channel, the only way in to the hidden sea for any sort of ocean-going vessel. Ice walls on either side of the channel rise up several hundred feet, straight up like the walls of a fjord . . ."

Then Erik remembered that other entry in his father's log:

"APRIL 25. The warm current of krill and the channel have disappeared. There is no sign of the whales.

"I put down the exact position of the channel, and we have returned to it. There is nothing here but empty sea, ice, and the broken walls of the ice mountains. Everything is frozen solid."

And there is no sign now, Erik thought. He unlimbered binoculars from the case strapped to the railing, and he looked again. There was no warm river of krill.

"Why have you lied to me?" Bornak asked. The veins swelled in his thick neck.

"A good question," Erik said. "You were going to certify me a great gunner, make me rich and famous. Why should I have lied to you, sir? The answer is that I would not—and I did not lie."

"Then where is the channel to the hidden sea?"

Erik said nothing. That terribly dry and cold wind whispered through the rigging and rippled the fur on Bornak's jacket.

"Erik, I'll still certify you as a gunner." Bornak tried without much success to soften his voice and give it a pleasant tone. "We will forget past differences, yah? We'll work together, find the sea, share the great hunt? I won't ask for your ten contract shots. Where's the hidden sea, Erik, and I'll sign your gunner's certificate now."

Erik looked past Bornak at the impenetrable walls of the ice barrier. "Why should I have lied to you?"

Bornak made a quick impatient jump at Erik, like an enraged bull. Then he stood uncertainly, clenching and unclenching his hands. "Yah," he finally said. "Why should you have lied? Nobody lies himself out of a chance to be great. But if you don't lie, where is the channel? If the hidden sea is close—where—?"

His voice rose above the wind. "I'll find it. I'll find it if I have to sail the Enderby Quadrant for ten years!"

Erik shook his head several times, unable to speak. He had thought of that other entry in his father's log, and the thought seemed to freeze his muscles.

"No—" he finally whispered. "You can't stay—"

"What?"

"We can't stay here, Bornak, any longer. Not even for an hour."

Bornak grabbed him and shook him. "You hold something back? What do you know? Tell me."

"April—" Erik said, his mouth dry. "April fourteen—"

"What of that?"

Erik started to blurt it out; then clamped his lips together. His father had found the channel into the hidden sea on April the twelfth. A day or so later the wind and the terrible freeze-up had come, and he'd had to run for his life:

". . . but the Enderby Sea doesn't cooperate with visitors," his father had written. "As we started to move in and begin shooting, we were hit by a ninety-mile-an-hour wind that struck like a thunderclap. And the temperature dropped at once to thirty below zero. The temperature kept dropping as we ran for our lives, and the sea itself began to freeze around us. We barely escaped toward the Scotia Sea and warmer waters . . ."

The same freeze-up was about to strike again. And if they didn't run for it now, and run hard, they would be caught.

But should he tell Bornak the truth? If he did, Bornak would take his crew out of the Enderby Sea to safety all right, before it was too late. But Bornak would also know the secret of the hidden sea. If he knew that, he would leave now for safe waters. But he would come back.

He would come back next season when he knew he'd find the channel open. He would still have his big hunt. It would still mean the final extinction of the blue whales.

It was a sad decision to have to make. But Erik hesitated only a moment. If it comes to that, he thought— if it's a choice between our survival or the whales'—why it has to be ours.

"April," Erik repeated in a flat grim tone. And he quickly explained everything to Bornak. In November and December, spring in Antarctica, the warm thawing river of krill opens the channel into the hidden sea. In

April, at the start of the Antarctic winter, the freeze-up begins: The terrible winds come; the channel is closed with pack ice—it disappears. Each season this pattern of thaw and freeze repeats itself, not at exactly, but at approximately the same time.

"That's what is happening now, Bornak. The big freeze has already started. The sea itself, my father said, will freeze—"

As Bornak listened, his eyes lit up. He started to grin. "That is the truth, all right. I see it. Yah, we have to run out of here now to escape the freeze. But in a few months it will be spring again, and we can come back, and the channel will be open and we can clean out the hidden sea of blues. We'll still have our big hunt, eh, Egil's son, and kill more blues than all other hunters put together?"

He hurried over to the phone and shouted down to McDun. "Rev up those engines. Schulstock, set your course. We're moving out. We're moving out, but we'll be coming back soon enough, you hear? We're coming back for the great hunt—"

Erik went below to the galley for coffee and a sandwich. He sat there a long time, listening to the wind. He knew he'd had no real choice.

TWENTY-THREE

The ice storm struck with terrible fury.

"Force 12," Schulstock said, the highest classification for wind velocity on the Beaufort scale. Over seventy knots, with a wind pressure of over seventeen pounds per square inch.

A bluish-black sky rushed in from the north, pouring over from the ice mountains like a great cloud of boiling smoke. With it swarmed a wilderness of icebergs and smaller ice clusters.

The engines labored to swing the catcher to port. Bornak was ordering Schulstock to pull in behind the nearest iceberg and use it as a partial shield against the wind.

Erik heard ice thundering and grinding through the fog as it crashed together and broke up. Waves fifty feet high boomed against the iceberg walls.

The mist and the spray started to freeze as they fell. A thickening pattern of ice quickly spread over the decks, masts, and lines.

The crew were soon only ghostly shapes in the mist as they fought the cold, inundating ice. They were issued axes, and they chopped frantically at the murderous stuff caking the upper rigging. "It could soon get too heavy," Tiburon had warned. Unless it was cleared, the catcher would carry a top-hamper that would roll it over to its doom.

With their ice axes, Erik and Tiburon climbed the port ratline leading up to the crow's nest, chopping desperately to right and left. Their breaths steamed around their faces as they worked in a murk so thick objects were hardly visible five feet away. Other crewmen chopped at the rigging above the superstructure, the stern mast, the lifeboats and rear superstructure, the smokestack and stays.

They worked their way back down toward the gunwale. Erik's face felt numb and raw. A sudden sharp *spanggggg* startled him. He stared at the splinter of steel gripped in his glove. The head had cracked and fallen from the ax handle.

It's already that cold, he thought, so cold it turns steel brittle enough to crack like glass.

He turned. A foot away stood Tiburon, his face and beard speckled with ice. He hunched nearer and shouted at Erik. "It's the big freeze rightly enough, Mr. Nordahl.

We're in too deep I think. That sea can freeze solid, close in, crush this ship like a walnut!"

When the shift changed, Tiburon sent Erik below for coffee and hot soup. On his way down to the galley, he noticed that the door to Bornak's cabin was open. Looking in, he saw Bornak hunched over the chart table. The ship's lantern swayed near a porthole that was completely covered with ice. Bornak looked up slowly at Erik in the dim light. He moved wearily, his eyes small and bloodshot. At that moment Erik heard a sudden cracking and grinding of ice about the catcher. He thought he saw a twitch of fear on Bornak's mouth as he started to push himself up from the chart table.

But the catcher shuddered, and a tremendous jolt hurled Bornak backward into the bulkhead.

His face turned pale as he sank to his knees near the collapsing frame of his steel bunk. Then he disappeared as though dissolving in a whirlpool. Erik stumbled through the doorway into the tilting cabin and felt himself hurled from one side of it to the other. Bulkheads and deck plates pounded his head and hands and body.

A black wind caught him. The bulkheads dissolved and the world faded into shadows. . . .

When Erik came to, he was lying just inside the opened steel doorway in Bornak's cabin. A second later he scrabbled wildly for a handhold as the deck of the cabin tilted at a forty-five-degree angle. The doorway was above him now still jammed open, and Bornak sinking below him against the opposite bulkhead.

The hull plates began to buckle and crack. The frosted glass of the porthole shattered inward. The entire length of the bulkhead split open.

Below him in the murk of the darkening, sea-flooding cabin Erik heard the gurgle of the water rushing in. He heard Bornak's muffled voice coming up as though from the depths of a well:

"Get topside, lad. Get out fast before the boilers blow!"

The sound of metal cracking ripped through the air. Erik tried to drag himself up out of the cabin through the doorway, but he kept slipping back down the sharply tilted, wet-slick deck. His arms lacked the strength to pull himself up, and his boots found no solid toehold on the deck plates.

Peering down, he barely made out the form of Bornak. The huge body was jammed down into the twisted wreckage of the cabin. He was grunting and trying to rise like the loser in a prizefight. The floor tilted down at a steeper angle. Erik, clinging weakly to the deck near the doorway, was now almost directly above the trapped Bornak who could not seem to extricate himself from the twisted metal. He looked up at Erik.

"Get out," he whispered. "Crawl on up—out that door . . . hurry . . ."

He raised one reddened hand toward Erik. His head

waggled, and his mouth worked with great effort. "Get out, lad—for God's sake—the boilers are going—save yourself—"

Erik clung to the tilting deck near the doorway and watched shards of ice pushing in through the catcher's steel hull as if the plates were wet cardboard. The needles were thick as a man. The catcher began to rock, held up by ice spindles, rock like a car on a Ferris wheel. Erik almost lost his hold—almost slid down the slanted deck into the freezing water with Bornak.

Lines of rivets trembled, bulged, and tore loose as more plating buckled. Water roared in through the cracks in the metal. The cabin was filling up rapidly with water laced with crushed ice.

Bornak looked at Erik with a bloody grin. Then he reached up with his huge hands, gripped Erik's ankles, and began lifting him an inch at a time toward the doorway. His massive shoulders bulged as he strained with Erik's weight. His huge arms swelled, and the veins squeezed above the surface.

Then as the water swirled over his face, Bornak hurled Erik up through the doorway and into the passageway leading aft.

Tiburon was yelling at him, helping him up the companionway toward the top deck. "The boilers. We've got to beat those boilers."

They felt their way sternward along a deck so steeply

angled that they had to hold to the port rail. Their boots kept slipping on the ice-slicked deck plates. The air was a wilderness of snow, racing past the catcher at close to eighty knots.

The ocean was thickening rapidly now. The water around the ship was already a deadly porridge of sea clutter freezing together into chunks of ice that rose fifty to a hundred feet around the catcher.

Narrow channels of sludge and water still flowed, but these channels, too, were rapidly narrowing. They would soon close. There would be no way out then.

A mass of ice cluster shaped like a huge fish was wedged in under the forward half of the catcher. Another cluster was closing in from the other side. The boat was caught in a pair of giant pincers.

The ship shivered. Its crushed forward half rose into the air, lifted high by the pincers.

"Where are the others?" Erik shouted.

"Several fools jumped onto a passing iceberg—didn't see just who. But they're fools to ride an iceberg here. Thousands of miles of empty sea clear to Cape Town. They'll never be picked up and the berg will melt . . ."

"Can we use the lifeboats?"

Tiburon pointed. The lifeboat to starboard was useless. But the port boat still hung from broken davits beside the stern superstructure. If they could loosen the boat and lower it in time, they might still get free of the catcher before the boilers blew.

Erik fought along the rail after Tiburon. The ice was lifting and twisting the foredecks higher out of the water, lowering the catcher's stern. It was as if the boat were being strangled, rivet by rivet, plate by plate.

As they reached the tilting lifeboat, there was a loud screech of plates and rending steel beams. The deck jolted over another foot. The lifeboat creaked and toppled to the side. Partly stunned and numbed with cold, Erik ducked and dodged pieces of flying ice as he fumbled at the lifeboat lashings. Tiburon worked at the line on the other end, barely visible now in the snow and foaming spindrift.

The boat was soon free but for two lines holding it fore and aft. Erik and Tiburon each gripped a line and eased the boat down and over the rail until it hung above the flowing sludge. They each had a line around the back and forward thwarts. Tiburon signaled, and they released both lines at once. The boat slapped down onto the sludge.

Thorder dragged Schulstock out toward the boat. Schulstock wore a bloody rag around his head, and he stared up into the snow.

As Erik held the lifeboat in hard to the catcher's hull, Tiburon and Thorder lowered Schulstock into it. Thorder dropped in after him.

Tiburon grabbed up the line from Erik. 'You're next, Mr. Nordahl.'' He called down to Thorder to grab an oar and fend off. Thorder pushed desperately against a hill of ice that was moving in, threatening to crush the boat into the catcher's hull.

"Get down there now, Mr. Nordahl," Tiburon said. He pushed Erik down into the boat, then jumped after him as Thorder snapped the painter loose and Erik snatched the other line free.

"Fend her off," Tiburon shouted to Thorder, who pushed with his oar against the pressing wall of ice. Erik grabbed up the other oar and pushed with everything left in him against the catcher's hull.

He shoved and strained against the stern section. It had twisted almost entirely away from the foredeck structure now. It was rolling hard over. Erik heaved with all his strength until the lifeboat was at oar's length. Then he got his oar into the lock quickly and sat down.

"Pull, pull!" Tiburon screamed at them through the wind. "Pull for your lives!"

Erik pulled. His shoulders seemed to tear from their sockets. But a few strong strokes put them beyond the range of the twisting stern section.

A few yards more, and the boilers blew.

Looking back, Erik saw a huge hole explode out of the entire midship's superstructure. Black smoke and flame shot up into the snow. The smokestack toppled to port.

The pincers of ice had been tearing the ship in half. The explosion finished the job. The stern now sagged. It turned and sank into the sludge, rolling like a dead whale. The sound was deafening.

"Pull, pull," Tiburon chanted hoarsely. "Pull hearty now."

Erik pulled and strained at the oars until his head spun and pain filled his chest. Inch by inch they managed to move through the thickening sludge.

Sometimes the ice clusters were only a few feet away. The sludge and the brash sea ice were everywhere.

Thorder pointed to the gelatinous mass around the boat. "It isn't getting any thinner—We're done for!"

"Pull, pull," Tiburon shouted. "Talking'll never get you to warm water."

"Aye."

"Pull, pull!"

They rowed until Erik had no feeling left in his body.

Once he looked back. The foredeck of the catcher had risen over thirty feet into the air. Erik saw the flared bow, the gun slanting upward, and the barbed head of the harpoon—and then all of it disappeared into swirls of mist . . .

Hours later—Erik never knew or cared how long— with Tiburon relieving first Thorder and then Erik at the oars, they had advanced some five miles. But they had cleared the worst of the sludge and could row a little faster.

Thorder sank down to the bottom of the boat beside

Schulstock, and his voice cracked with fatigue and hope-
lessness. "A lifeboat lost in this devil's sea! We don't
have the chance of carps among shark."

"I think we have a chance, don't you, Mr. Nordahl?"
said Tiburon.

"I think we do, bosun." Erik gave a tired but happy
grin. "And we're not exactly lost, Thorder."

"You know where we are?" Thorder muttered.

"No, but we know which way to set our course," Erik
said.

"Aye," Tiburon said. "The pack ice."

"Right," Erik said. "We could beat our way along the
edge of the pack ice to the Sandwich Islands in a boat
like this, if we had to."

"If we clear the sludge," Thorder groaned.

"Shackleton survived seven hundred and fifty miles
in an ordinary open ship's boat," Tiburon said. "Right
here in the Antarctic. Right, Mr. Nordahl?"

"I think he did that, bosun."

"None of us are blasted Shackletons," Thorder said.
But he took over the oar again, and Tiburon sat at the
bow of the boat. Thorder rowed hard then and said no
more about never getting out.

And hours later open water appeared, clear except for
big icebergs and lines of broken pack ice, all drifting
fast in a powerful current, under the dark sky.

Tiburon and Erik got the small sail on then. They
tugged the halyards and ran up the foresail, a bright

ocher-colored rag that was enough for a while in the strong wind. Later Erik whipped up the mainsail while Tiburon held the tiller.

"We'll start beating back into the wind now, Mr. Nordahl," Tiburon said. "There's plenty of room to tack her. Navigation's no problem, is it?"

"Not much of one," Erik said. "Just keep to the edge of the pack ice. Keep it always on our port. We're bound to sail northeast sooner or later into the Scotia Sea."

They had good wind and bearable weather, and they reached the Scotia Sea four days later. Tiburon got in touch with Gunner Captain Trasti's *Catcher Four* as soon as it was in range, using the emergency shortwave radio with which the lifeboat was equipped. After that they kept sending out direction signals and they waited to be picked up by Trasti.

The thought of the approaching catcher and his return to the fleet sobered Erik. Tiburon saw his troubled look. "The season isn't over, Mr. Nordahl. I'll tell Captain Haakonsson what happened. You can still get your chance at the whales. There's still time for those ten contract shots. Do you want them? Do you want to try again?"

Erik thought about Tiburon's question.

Maybe he still wanted to shoot whales. Maybe he didn't. He might end up not being any sort of whaleman at all.

But he was sure of one thing now. He knew the answer to something that had puzzled him and hurt him for many years. He knew why his father had kept him in school until he was sixteen, instead of taking him out on a catcher when he was nine and raising him in *Zuther Notion,* the way most gunners did with their sons. The way Bornak's father had done.

Erik knew that if he had been killing whales since he was nine years old, he would probably have ended up like Bornak. He would never have known there was anything else in the world but killing whales. He would never have questioned the killing of whales. Worse, he would never have known, or even suspected, that he might have wanted to be something else besides a whale killer.

But now he knew, from those sixteen years of school and study, that there were many other worlds than the one you could see from the bow of a whale catcher. His father had kept him away from the sea and the whales at least long enough for him to be able to think, to choose and act for himself.

He smiled at Tiburon, but he didn't answer him. Instead, he looked ahead into the wind, and waited for the smoke of Trasti's catcher to appear on the far horizon of the Scotia Sea.

ABOUT THE AUTHOR

Bryce Walton's interest in whales began on a fishing boat off the coast of Baja California, where he first saw the tremendous creatures, seventy and eighty feet long, playing joyously in the waves with schools of dolphins. Whales, he was told, belong to the same family of warm-blooded mammals as dolphins and are just as playful, friendly, courageous, and intelligent. He knew that whales were hunted as sources of oil and bonemeal, and he began to wonder what it meant to kill them. He did a great deal of research, reading about the animals and talking with marine biologists and with men who had hunted the remarkable blue and finback whales of the Antarctic. The result is this book, about a young man who finds out, as Mr. Walton says, "what it is like to shoot a dolphin as big as a house."

The author has been a sailor, a gold miner, and a college instructor in short-story writing, though for many years he has devoted all of his time to writing. In 1961 he won the Alfred Hitchcock Best Short Story of the Year Award.

Born in Blythedale, Missouri, Mr. Walton studied English literature and drama at Los Angeles City College. As a combat correspondent during World War II, he received a special citation for his coverage of the battle of Iwo Jima.

He now lives in Brooklyn with his wife and spends much of his leisure time sailing, skin diving, and spelunking. His first book for young people, *Cave of Danger*, was published in 1967.